THE CARRIER'S DILEMMA

Bite of Magic – Book 4

LUCILLE YATES

Book and Cover design by Maria Spada
Edits by Owl Eyes Proofs & Edits
Book Formatting Template by Derek Murphy @Creativindie

First Edition: March 2023

Print ISBN: 9781961142039
eBook ISBN: 9781961142022

Kitty Hex Press

www.lucilleyateswrites.com

DEDICATION

To Elizabeth.

Thank you for your support, for helping me brainstorm,

and for being you. Please don't change.

CHAPTER 1

Mornings after working the third shift at the emergency vet left Emma exhausted. Still, she found herself sitting at Gallery Espresso across from Maggie five minutes after it opened. She could hear her bed calling to her, but her past self agreed to this early morning coffee meeting.

Maggie looked bleary-eyed herself. She lacked any eye makeup, and it didn't look like she'd brushed her hair. Her bright pink pixie cut stood straight up in the back, and the front looked glued to her forehead.

"Why are you doing this?" Emma laid her head down on the table between them with a moan. "It's too early. Or too late. Pick one."

Maggie's fingers scratched the back of Emma's head. It felt nice. Surely, Gallery Espresso wouldn't mind if Emma took a nap.

"We wanted to talk about what we thought of the

plans Aunt S and Uncle E came up with." She stopped scratching Emma's head. "And your schedule is a bit chaotic at the moment."

Emma propped her head on her hand. She had started covering for as many people as possible between the veterinarian's office and the emergency vet clinic over the past month. She wanted to return all the favors she'd called in over the past six months.

Ever since Cernunnos's hunters began attacking her wolf pack, The Old Moss Pack, and the local witch coven Maggie belonged to, The Midnight Oak Coven, she'd had too many people covering for her at work. Nothing says doctor of veterinary medicine like skipping out on work.

"You should stop working such crazy hours." Maggie took a sip of her tea. "Surely you've paid everyone back for covering you."

A groan escaped Emma. "I have, but now I'm working on increasing everyone's good graces. Who knows when I'll need to go help the family again?"

It sounded like they were in the mafia, but it became their code for helping the Old Moss Wolf Pack or the Moonlight Oak Coven.

The irony wasn't lost on Emma how both she and Maggie belonged to groups, despite not having the skills for either. Maggie didn't have any natural magic, and even though Emma had better hearing and eyesight than an average human, she couldn't shift into a wolf, not even during the full moon.

"Don't run yourself into the ground."

"I won't, Mom," Emma stuck her tongue out.

Maggie smirked. "I'm the world's most mysterious mom. How did I have a child before I was born? It's my biggest secret."

"I'm not here to discuss the applications of impossible magic. I want to know how you feel about waiting."

Maggie reached into her bag and pulled out a green spiral notebook and flipped to the page she marked with a sticky note. She pushed the notebook over to Emma and scooted closer. "According to my research, Baldy has all but two of the books he needs. So right now, they have two targets, which might explain why they aren't coming after us constantly."

She pointed to a location in her rough sketch of North America. "One dictionary is located around here." She pointed to a location near Toronto, Canada. "Now, even if S says we don't have the other one, I still don't believe her."

By 'S,' Maggie meant her Aunt Sylvia, the leader of the coven. They started speaking in code over the last few months when alone in case anyone was listening in, and it helped when they were in public. They called Cernunnos Baldy because the guy in charge had a very close haircut. Really, at that length, he may as well just shave it all off.

Dictionaries were the books the organization was searching for. Old books of knowledge that belonged to five covens. Each book contained a piece of a spell which, when put together, would suck the magic out of everything and everyone, giving it all to one person. At least that was the story.

"Did you talk to anyone there?" Emma pointed at Toronto on the map.

"Yes, but not for long. S talked to them first. And no, they won't destroy the book or the page with the information. Apparently, it's more complicated than tearing a page out and burning it." Her fingers drummed on the table. Emma looked at her watch.

Finger drumming time started at 7:46 am. She liked to see how long Maggie would keep drumming her fingers. She watched Maggie drop her pinky first, followed by the other three in quick succession after it. The fluid movement threatened to lull her to sleep.

"Where else can we look for your dictionary?" Emma asked, still focused on the moving fingers.

"S's house. Under floorboards or in the walls, probably. We've looked everywhere else." Maggie stuck out her bottom lip. She didn't normally pout, but when she did, she looked like a teenager, especially with bright pink hair surrounding her face. Thank the gods she dyed it back. She dyed it dark brown a few months ago in an attempt to throw off the bounty hunters Cernunnos sent after her. The dark brown looked terrible on her. It shocked Emma every time she saw her, and she'd helped dye it that god awful brown color.

"Does she have a safe deposit box?"

Maggie's fingers stopped. "That might be easier to get into than her house."

Emma laughed and looked down at her watch. 7:48. Only two minutes of anxious tapping.

"Have you found out anything from E?" Maggie yawned.

E or Ethan was the pack leader. "No. I don't know why they keep me around. It's like he doesn't trust me. It's frustrating. I just want to help."

"They keep you around because you do everything. You fight better than the rest of them, without claws and teeth." Maggie sat back and took a sip of her drink. "Remember when we were little, and we'd read whatever we could get our hands on?"

Emma nodded and thought of the days they would lie in her father's study poring over his books on were-creatures or sitting in the corner of Maggie's Gigi's shop going through her craft books. Both of them were trying to overcompensate for things they couldn't control.

"Remember that book on Princeps Luporum?"

"Yes, I do," Emma said. "I was obsessed with it for almost a year. You were so sick of me coming up with ideas of what I would do if I were the Princeps Luporum."

"Ruler of the wolves, Prince Emma." Maggie lifted her cup up.

Emma did as well, and they clinked their coffee cups together in a toast. Even though princeps in Latin means anything from ruler to chief, Maggie liked the sound of Prince. She thought it was funny all those years ago and apparently, she still did.

"I just wanted to feel important. Of course, being able to shift would be nice and to have a solid color coat? That's still a dream. The shifting part, not the solid coat part."

"Which color would you want now? Snow white fur or midnight black fur?"

"Black. Easier to be sneaky, sneaky."

Maggie chuckled. "How we have changed over the years."

"Yeah. Back to the topic. Maybe you can get Chuck to help."

"Chuckers?" Maggie's pitch rose in surprise. "He shouldn't help me with that. Besides, they left today. It'll be a good..." Maggie paused and scrunched up one side of her face, thinking. "Eight or nine days till they get back."

Chuck was dating Maggie's cousin Jesi, and they had gone on a ten-day cruise.

"Oh yeah. I forgot about that. We should go on a cruise."

"We should go on a cruise. After this dictionary mess is over, it's cruise time." Maggie's eyes lit up. "We'd be the hottest bitches there. No one would be safe from our sexual... energy."

"You could get laid here."

"That is zero fun. We need a chance to get away from this crazy year. Get out there and spread our—"

"Legs?" Emma cut in with a snort.

"Not what I was going to say, but we can stick with that. It's a much different image than wings." She grinned. "Now I'm imagining someone flying, but instead of wings on their back, their legs are flapping. Two pairs of legs, one in the normal spot and the other pair off the back."

"That's a cursed image. How dare you share it?" She laughed with her best friend. Maybe staying up a little longer after a long shift wasn't so bad.

Maggie turned the page in her notebook and began to draw. Emma's eyes widened, then she reached across the table to snatch the pencil and paper away from her. "We don't actually need to see it."

"It'll just be in stick figure form," Maggie said between giggles.

Emma pulled the two objects out of her friend's hands with a deep breath, then paused.

The scent of cedarwood mixed with jasmine froze her on the spot. A note of vanilla followed the other two aromas. Something in her chest rumbled, and her pulse quickened.

She dropped the notebook and pencil and swiveled in her chair. Where exactly was the smell coming from? Somewhere behind the partition that separated the seating area from the coffee bar held the answer. She stood up, knocking her chair over. Maggie said something, but Emma ignored her as she floated away from the table.

Chapter 2

Jack

The walk to the coffee shop took longer than Jack had patience for. If only the high-end hotel he had stayed at provided quality coffee, he wouldn't be walking across downtown Savannah so early in the morning. Well, two blocks isn't really across the city, but it felt like it at the moment.

He could hear his sister's voice in his head now. "You are such a coffee snob." With a scoff, he would answer with, "I'm a coffee connoisseur." It reminded him of the mug she bought him a few years ago that said "Coffee Snob" on the side. He would never tell her, but it was his favorite. Mostly because it held sixteen ounces of liquid, but also the mug was accurate.

The coffee shop looked like a damn shiny castle in front of him, the Gallery Espresso. It was a beacon of light at the end of his coffee-less morning. The person at the front desk told him they made some of the best coffee in the city. Anything would be better after the mud the hotel tried to pass off as coffee.

A strong java scent wafted through the door as it opened and closed with customers leaving, their hands full of cups of joe. He pushed through the door and made his way to the counter. Luckily, no one was in line, and he ordered a large black coffee. When they called his name, he wrapped his large hands around the cup and inhaled the scent. A moan almost escaped his mouth. He couldn't hold back the moan once he took a sip of the sweet nectar. Maybe Savannah wouldn't be so bad after all. He took another sip and made his way to the door.

Paul, his co-worker, expected him to tag along to his meeting with the city regarding zoning and site development. These meetings could take more than a week before the company could officially buy the lot they want for the hotel. Of course, Jack couldn't care less about all of that. He was here as the face of the brand and to work on his own project.

He needed to find one person who could lead him to his best friend. And that person happened to be somewhere in Savannah. The thought of dividing his time between his search and the hotel aggravated him. If only his sister was free to do the face of the business portion. She's the one who wanted the hotel division of the business. He preferred the part that provided more impact on the community.

Another sip brought him closer to rational, and he made his way to the exit. Time to go back and get dressed for the day. Going to meetings in shorts got him in trouble with Paul and the CEO, his sister.

Too focused on the door, he didn't notice the person who stepped in front of him. They slammed into each other. His coffee, his glorious coffee, spilled over the cup onto his hands and his clothes, burning the shit out of him. He looked up, words of anger on his tongue.

"I'm so sorry," she said. Big brown eyes stared up at him. Red filled her cheeks, and her lips formed an 'o' shape.

"No," he said, "it's my fault. I wasn't looking where I was going. Are you hurt?"

Her green scrubs were free of coffee. The clothes did nothing to hide her wide hips or her defined arms. Her long brown hair pulled back into a ponytail showed off a single cartilage piercing in her left ear.

She was exactly what Jack didn't need, but exactly what he wanted.

"Let me get you another drink," he said.

Her deep laugh warmed him more than the coffee. "I'm pretty sure it's your drink that spilled. I've finished my drink. Let me buy you another one."

"I'll let you buy me another coffee, if you'll let me take you to lunch."

He didn't know why he just asked her out. It might have something to do with him not wanting to look away.

~

Emma

She could still smell him over the spilled coffee. Cedar with hints of jasmine and vanilla filled her nose. Her wolf, who rarely came forward, who she thought didn't exist until her father died, panted in between yipping the word mate in her head. Part of her wanted to roll her eyes because she figured it out without her silly wolf, but the other part felt too enamored with the man in front of her.

He was tall, taller than her brother, with brown hair, half sticking up, and gray eyes that bored into hers. Light stubble graced his face and she wanted to reach out to touch it.

"Sure, I can have lunch with you," she said, holding her hand out. "I'm Emma."

A voice whispered behind her, so softly only her wolf hearing could pick it up. "You're working third shift. Try dinner instead." Maggie walked past with her neon pink hair. The man in front of her didn't even look at Maggie.

"Jack." He shook Emma's hand, causing her heart to skip a beat.

"Let's get you another coffee." She motioned toward the counter. "But I just remembered I can't have lunch. I'm working an odd shift this week. Breakfast and dinner are open, though."

As they walked, she tried not to look too eager, but it didn't quite work as she couldn't stop looking at him, the beauty mark behind his left ear, or his full lips.

"Dinner works. Can you meet me here tonight at seven?"

"I'll meet you right out front. Seven o'clock sharp."

Her wolf nudged her to grab him and run as Emma paid for his coffee. It's not the best time to learn about her wolf's irrational side.

His smile warmed her from the inside. "Well," he said, "I need to go get changed. I have a meeting."

"Oh, yeah. Of course." She stepped back and watched him walk out the door. He smiled and waved, then stopped and turned around to walk in the other direction.

Maggie laughed beside her, causing her to jump. "I like him," Maggie said. "He likes you enough to forget where he's going."

That thought made Emma smile. She liked that he couldn't keep his eyes off her and asked to see her again.

"What I don't understand is why you're looking at him like that." Maggie's narrowed eyes locked on Emma.

"Like what?" She had played this game before. Being best friends, they rarely kept anything from the other. As much as she wanted to keep Jack to herself for a bit, she knew she couldn't keep it from Maggie. Mostly because she was there and watched it all happen.

"Like you want to chase after him. Like you want to lick him all over. Like you want to find a nice quiet corner and—"

"You've made your point," Emma said with her hand over Maggie's grinning mouth. She took her hand away before it got licked. "Walk me to my car."

Maggie wiggled while she walked beside Emma. "You like him," she sang.

"Okay, fine." Emma grabbed her bestie's arm and pulled her close. "He's my mate."

"What?" Maggie yelled. The hand tightening around her arm didn't quiet Maggie down. "That guy? He's cute, but you could do better."

"Shh, you crazy lady." The street wasn't a place to yell. She did not need the extra attention. Too many humans lived, well, everywhere. They didn't need a breach of magical secrecy if Maggie got too excited.

"Fate disagrees with you." The lock on her car door opened when she pressed the key fob in her pocket. "And I will not pass him up. I didn't even think I'd have a mate."

"Ridiculous. Of course, you'd have a mate."

"I'm a carrier, not a full..." she looked around them, then whispered, "wolf or human."

"You've always been more wolf than human." Maggie talked under her breath, but Emma still heard her.

She decided to be the mature one and stuck her tongue out at Maggie.

"Go home and rest up for your big date." Maggie said big date in a breathy voice followed by sticking her own tongue out, only she folded her tongue in a weird clover shape.

The door shut before she could tell Maggie her tongue looked weird, but Maggie already knew. It's why she did it. The smile stayed on Emma's face when she pulled out of her parking spot and headed home. Having a mate settled her. Gave her a sense of belonging. Growing up, being the only werewolf that couldn't shift gave her a bit of a complex she tried to ignore.

Her father's voice popped into her head. "You are the sum of yourself, not the sum of what others see or expect. Your only competition is who you look at in the mirror every day. Don't listen to what the others say. Being a werewolf is more than just shifting. It's an attitude. It's smell, strength, and community."

Finding her mate shouldn't give her a sense of confirmation, but she'd never felt more connected to her wolf. By the time she pulled into her driveway, exhaustion took over. In a few hours, she'd be back with her mate, so she relaxed into her bed and slept.

C h a p t e r 3

Jack

Paul wasn't happy when Jack skipped out on dinner with a few of the government officials. Logically, getting involved with someone in a town hundreds of miles away from his own was a bad idea. That didn't stop him from standing in front of The Gallery Espresso. He'd thought about Emma all day. Something about her grabbed his attention, from her soft brown eyes to her potent presence.

"Jack."

He turned to find Emma walking toward him. She wore brown slacks with a blue sleeveless blouse that showed off her toned arms. Long brown hair flowed behind her back like a cape. A smile graced her gorgeous face, and he couldn't stop his response.

"Emma," he said before he leaned down and kissed her cheek. The move felt right, even though they had only met that morning.

A light pink flushed her cheeks for a moment before her hand wrapped under his elbow.

"So, where are we going?" She looked up at him. He stood at six two, but she wasn't too much shorter than him.

"There's a restaurant a short walk from here that someone recommended." Jack closed his hand around her hand that rested on his arm. He asked that same employee who pointed him to Gallery Espresso for a dinner recommendation. If this worked out, he'd give the guy a tip and a good word to the manager.

"Are you going to leave me in suspense, or are you going to tell me?"

He led her across the street to the square. "I enjoy leaving you in suspense."

"At least let me guess." She stood up straighter. "I'm great at guessing games."

"Really?"

"No. But that's why it's fun." Her grin gave his stomach butterflies.

"Far be it from me to take away such joy. Guess away."

She looked around before he led her across the street again. "We're headed north. Which means we're walking away from Six Pence and Fire Street Food. Up ahead we can turn to go to the Thai place, an Italian bistro, or barbeque. If we make it all the way to Broughton, I might have to give up."

"It's before Broughton."

"Are you going to walk us in a large circle and bring us back to The Public? That's something Maggie would do."

"Who's Maggie?"

"She's my best friend. She was with me this morning. It's hard to miss her with her bright pink hair."

"I don't remember anyone with pink hair this morning."

She stopped them on the sidewalk. "You don't remember seeing anyone with neon pink hair?"

He couldn't read her face, but he wanted to. Did he see shock or amusement? Maybe both. "I really don't remember."

A smile slowly grew on her lips. She turned and continued walking. "Interesting."

He laughed. "Anyway, I wouldn't walk you in a giant circle. Not at the beginning of the date."

"Is that right?"

"Yep. Circles come later when I'm trying to delay the inevitable. The end of the evening." They reached the other side of Oglethorpe Avenue, and he turned left.

"What makes you think you won't run screaming out of the restaurant in the middle?" She asked.

"If I run screaming, that means I've had an eventful night and might consider doing it again."

Her laugh was loud and full. She didn't try to hide it or her bright smile. "I now have goals."

He stopped in front of the restaurant and opened the door. "Here we are."

She tilted her head and smirked. "Husk? I'd forgotten

about this place. It's good." Before she walked through the door, she winked.

Once he gave his name to the hostess to check his reservation, the hostess walked them through the converted home to a rustic-looking table for two. He barely registered the simple yet elegant place settings. His eyes stayed on Emma. Her hair swished behind her, but it framed her face in the front.

She leaned forward with her elbow on the table. "So, tell me, Jack. Everything."

He laughed. "That's a tall order. How about we start with something small? How long have you lived in the area?"

"My entire life." She leaned back in her chair. "My brother lives here as well as most of the friends of the family. What about you?"

"I'm here on business. I'm from Winston-Salem." He didn't have to wait long for her eyes to widen in surprise.

"Winston-Salem? That's not exactly close. What brings you to the low country and how long are you staying?" Her surprised expression disappeared as quickly as it appeared.

"I work for a company that's trying to build a hotel in the area. I'm learning from the person in charge of the project, and I don't know how long I'll be in town. Anywhere from one to four weeks depending on negotiations. Paul insists on handling everything in person."

"I'm very glad he does."

"Me too. What about you? You were wearing scrubs

this morning." He leaned forward, his forearms on the table.

"I'm a veterinarian. I'm working the night shift at the emergency clinic this week. There's a group of vets that rotate that shift to help the emergency vet clinic. So, you have until about ten o'clock to walk me in circles."

"Plenty of time for you to scare me away." He winked.

"I'm not sure where the challenge lies now," Emma said with a smirk. "Should I make you stay or scream?"

"Hello, welcome to Husk," the server said, causing Jack to jump. "My name is Wesley, and I'll be your server."

"Hey Wes. I didn't know you were working here."

"I've worked here for a year. I can't believe you didn't know. We only see each other every month." The tall, thin waiter rolled his eyes at Emma but turned with a smile toward Jack. "Here's our menu. If you have any questions, please let me know. What can I get you to drink?"

"Just water for me," Jack said with a smile.

"Me too." Emma grinned at Jack as Wesley walked away. "He's one of the many family friends. We were in most of the same classes growing up."

"So, I should corner him for all the good stories?"

She smirked. "Sure. He'd have some good stories. Ask away."

"That means he doesn't have any dirt. What was your best friend's name again?"

"She'd never betray me."

"Your brother might. I know I'd talk to embarrass my sister."

"A true sibling. Do you just have the one?" Emma leaned back in her chair.

"Yes. She's the oldest and most responsible, or rather has the most ambition. She knows exactly what she wants." He thought about how much he used to envy his sister's drive to succeed. Along the way, he learned everyone had a unique vision of success.

"So, you don't know what you want?"

"Oh, I know. It's just less corporate."

"'Cause hotels aren't corporate at all. Quite the opposite. I believe they're non-profits, right?"

"Wow. You're kind of an ass." He laughed. Their conversation came easy, like they'd known each other for years.

"I have a nice ass, yes."

Wesley placed the waters down at that moment. "I don't want to know. Are you ready to order?"

"I'm ready if you are," Emma said with a raised eyebrow at him.

"I'll get whatever she's having."

"Living dangerously. What will it be, Emma?" The server asked.

"Shrimp and grits, please."

"You got it." He took their menus as he left the table.

"Yes, I work for a hotel company. Same as my sister, but she's the CEO, and I'm going from position to position as a favor for her. There are some days she treats me like her second set of eyes."

"Your sister is the CEO of a hotel corporation?"

He froze because he never planned on telling her his actual connection to Bellamy Hotels. He hated the shift in people when they found out he had tons of money, not that he used much of it on himself. Past relationships never worked out because he ended up with superficial people. But he'd already let it out of the bag.

"Yeah. She's done a great job so far. She's less distracted than the last CEO."

Emma's happy demeanor fell as she stared at him. A single finger tapped the table, and she narrowed her eyes.

"I'm trying to decide if I want to know or not. I want to know, but it doesn't seem important. But it is also where you work." She leaned back in her chair and crossed her arms. "I'll think about it."

He laughed. No one ever reacted that way, as if asking would put a strain on the relationship. And they were only on the first date.

"It's Bellamy Hotels."

Her eyes widened. "That's one fancy hotel. Your sister is awesome. CEO of the fanciest hotel I've ever stepped foot in and it was only the lobby."

"You've never stayed there? Just went into the lobby?"

"That is accurate. Maggie and I walked around the downstairs of the one in Myrtle Beach once. How old is your sister? I thought all CEOs were old fogies."

"Well, she's overqualified for the job and the old CEO retired. She was next in line and wanted the job."

"Next in line?" she frowned. "Wait. Are you a Bellamy?"

"Um… yeah." He rubbed the back of his neck.

"Oh."

"And you don't want to be a big shot hotel mogul?"

"I really don't."

"Fascinating." She leaned on the table again. "What is it you want to do instead?"

This question he couldn't answer. How should he tell the woman beside him that he wants to continue the other half of his family's legacy? He'd never wanted to explain his real desire to a date before now. But how does someone explain the supernatural to another human? It would be much easier if he was supernatural. He would at least have something to show her.

"I want to be a mediator. Help two people or parties find common ground. But I keep getting pulled into the hotel business." He fell back onto his practiced answer easily but felt the burn of guilt in his chest.

"Wow. That's a hard job."

"It can be rewarding when you help find a solution between parties."

"That's much more interesting than hotels."

"The only thing I want to do with hotels is pick out their coffee."

"Coffee?"

"I'm a bit of a coffee connoisseur, and Morgan, my sister, likes to buy local coffee to serve at the hotels."

"You have a side quest for coffee this visit as well, huh?"

"That's the plan. You know of any good places?"

"Of course. I might agree to accompany you."

"I'll call you when I have the time."

By then, Wes placed their food in front of them. It smelled delicious. Jack's mouth watered. He looked up and smiled at Emma.

"This better be good."

She scoffed and laughed. "I didn't make it. This is just my go to dish. It's like my caliber to know how good a restaurant is."

She took a big bite of the shrimp and grits in front of her and moaned. The warm sound went straight to his groin. Sounds like that never affected him before.

He dug in before he could get more worked up. The shrimp was spicy on his tongue. Mixed with the grits, cheese, and gravy it made him moan at how good it tasted. Food should never be this delicious. And watching Emma eat, hearing the sounds she made, had him squirming in his seat. He already knew he wanted a second date.

~

Emma

Dinner with Jack was perfect, if she didn't count Wes glancing their way every five minutes. The entire pack would know about her date before it ended. She felt self-conscious after she moaned while taking her first bite of food, but she saw his reaction through her eyelashes and couldn't stop herself from continuing. She liked how she affected him. To be honest, she felt the same way. His lovely mouth wrapped around that fork would look even better on her nipples.

She declined dessert. She'd rather spend time walking around with him than eating. On the way out of the restaurant while she waited for Jack to come back from the bathroom, Wes whispered in her ear. "Have fun on your mate-date."

She stared at him wide eyed. "What? Why would you…"

"Oh, I can tell by how you look at him. Think he has a brother he'd let me borrow?" He winked.

"He has a sister."

Wes pursed his lips. "Not really my preference."

"You can't tell anyone about the mate part. I…" she let go of the breath she was holding. "It should come from me."

"Spoilsport. Fine. Text me when I'm allowed to gossip." He looked over her shoulder. "Now go claim him."

"Ready?" Jack asked.

"Thank you for dining with us today. Be sure to visit again. Good night." Wes blew Emma a kiss and went back to work.

"I'm ready." She put her hand through his arm and led him outside.

"He's… interesting." Jack didn't look back as he spoke.

"He is. But I'd rather hear more about you."

Emma smiled up at Jack, and his shoulders relaxed.

"What do you want to hear?"

"Everything, of course. Let's start with movies and why your favorite is secretly rom coms."

His laugh did something to her tummy.

"I do like rom coms. I like to laugh and enjoy the happily ever after. Fantasy is also a favorite. Some of them are hilarious."

"Fantasies are hilarious?"

"Of course. People's interpretations of cryptids are very amusing."

"An unbeliever!" Emma cried. "You're in Savannah. We have ghosts everywhere. You'll go home haunted if you say that too loud."

"I can handle a ghost. No worries."

"Sounds like you need to go on a ghost tour."

"As long as it's with you, I'll go anywhere."

They walked around downtown for the next hour. They talked like they had known each other for years. All the while, Emma felt the pull to expose her deepest secret and a pull to finish the bond with him. With his easy laughs and flirty tones, would it all disappear when he learned about the supernatural?

But she held back. The secrets could wait. To complete the bond, they would need to have intercourse, but she would never force him into a bond without his permission, even if it would be the best sex of her life. She wanted to enjoy this for a while. By the end of the date, she slowed their pace on the way back to her car.

"I've really enjoyed tonight," she said.

"Is that why we're walking so slow?"

"Yeah. Wanna come to work with me?" She gave him a big grin, not caring that it showed off her canines.

"Do I get to help with the animals or are you asking to play doctor with me?" The glint in his eyes looked dangerous and oh so inviting.

"Yes." She giggled. Damnit. She actually giggled. She never giggled. Belly laugh, snort, snicker? Of course, but giggle? Never.

"I'd like to do this again," she said, stopping beside her car. "This is me."

"I'd like to do this again too."

"How about you meet me Thursday, tomorrow night?"

"I'll need to check the schedule. Paul, my co-worker, has a way of adding stuff to the calendar."

"Okay. Here," she handed him her phone. "Give me your number."

He added his number, and she sent him a text. "Now you can let me know." She smirked at him and put her hands on his chest. He felt solid under her palms.

Warm hands landed on her hips, and he pulled her a little closer. "I'd like to kiss you," he whispered.

"I'd like that too."

She leaned up before he could move and pressed her lips to his and wrapped her arms around his neck. The warmth of his lips spread down her spine. A moan similar to the one she made at dinner escaped her. His hands traveled up her back and pulled her close. They both opened their mouths as one. He tasted as good as he smelled. Her body responded by melting against his. The feel of his soft hair through her fingers and the strength of his embrace settled her soul. They were here together, their tongues meeting in a deep kiss, and her wolf howled for joy in her head. All she desired stood before her and she never wanted to let go.

All too soon, Jack pulled away from the kiss. His lips looked pink and swollen, his hair tousled from her grip. She leaned against her car and briefly wondered when that happened.

"You probably need to leave," he said, resting his forehead against hers.

"I don't wanna." The whine left her mouth before she could stop it.

Warm hands cupped her cheek. "I know. I don't want you to either."

She took a deep breath. "I really should go."

"I'll message you."

"I'll hold you to it."

"I should warn you; I don't follow the standard rules for dating."

She leaned back and eyed him up and down. "Meaning?"

"I won't wait three days to text. I'll probably message you in the morning."

"I can work with that."

She kissed his lips softly once more, then slid out of his arms and into her car.

C h a p t e r   4

Jack

Jack walked toward Bay Street. He was running a bit late. Paul insisted on afternoon drinks with someone. He couldn't remember if the person they met was part of the city council or the owner of a construction company. Schmoozing tended to ruin his day. But not today. Today, he had plans with Emma. She wanted to show him around River Street.

So far, at least five people told him the city had open container laws in the historic district, and his only goal was to not drink too much. He shared too much when he drank in excess, excess being between three to four drinks. Drunkenly telling people about the supernatural ended poorly.

As he approached Bay Street, he spotted Emma across the road in front of a short wrought-iron fence. The intricately designed fence encircled a patch of green with a lion fountain in the middle. He was a bit confused when she had said to meet her at the lion, but she assured him it would make sense once he got there.

Her face lit up when she noticed him on the crosswalk. She wore jeans and a black t-shirt, both snug, emphasizing her wide hips and round rear. It reminded him that he wanted to take her dancing, just to feel her ass grind against him.

He hurried across the road and embraced her in a tight hug. The scent of her hair made him pull her closer. Too soon, they broke away with her kissing his cheek.

"So, what do you think?" She motioned toward the fountain.

"It's lovely. Is that terra cotta?" The red-winged lion sat on the edge of the fountain spitting water out of its mouth.

"It was terra cotta until someone ran it over. Now it's painted concrete. If it's hit by another car, it'll leave a good dent this time."

He looked at her when she placed her hand in the crook of his arm. Light brown eyes looked into his. She pulled him along the street and began pointing out buildings and telling stories. Her smile entranced him as they walked. The tour took them down to River Street, where she pointed out her favorite stores and the cargo ships as they floated by.

The conversation flowed between them. Some people were meant to be friends. She talked about the animals she treated while he talked about the pets he'd had as a kid. Soon their conversation turned into crazy childhood antics.

"I swear we would go out behind my house and practice throwing knives. That stopped when my brother told on us because our aim was better than his. Apparently, that was an adult supervised activity."

"I'm sure you got your revenge."

Emma laughed. "Oh yeah. I hid all his guitar picks around the house. I can still throw better than him, though."

"Really?"

"I'm an expert at throwing shit."

"I'd like to see that. Emma, thrower of knives and shit."

"There's an ax throwing place in town if you want to see."

He smiled at her one-hundred-watt grin. "Let's do it. We can make it a competition."

"Perfect. I enjoy winning."

He laughed as she pulled him along the cobblestone road. The more time he spent with her, the more he realized how much he didn't want to leave her. He was helplessly swept up in the moment, even if she led him to his demise.

"Emma," someone yelled. Emma turned and frowned a little before replacing it with a half-smile. A tall, lean man with brown hair and holey jeans walked up to her with a wave.

"Hey Spencer." She dropped Jack's hand.

He felt the loss of connection immediately. She crossed her arms over her chest, cocking her hips to the side. Her actions didn't seem to have any effect on the newcomer. Jack moved to her side, but refrained from touching her.

"Whatcha doin'?" Spencer asked Emma while looking at Jack.

"About to get dinner. What are you doing?" Emma raised an eyebrow. Jack was content to watch.

"We were checking out a new venue. Where are you going to eat?" Spencer looked between him and Emma, then stared at Emma with wide eyes.

"No," Emma said.

"No?"

"No, you cannot come to dinner with us."

"So, there is an us." Spencer grinned.

In that moment, it struck Jack that his grin favored Emma's. This must be her brother. He glanced at her just as she looked over at him. The small shrug he gave her must have cemented her decision because in that moment she sighed.

"Spencer, this is Jack. Jack, this is my brother Spencer."

"It's a pleasure to meet you." Jack stuck out his hand.

Spencer clasped Jack's hand in a quick but firm handshake. "It's nice to meet you, Jack. Tell me, do you like dogs?"

Emma swatted Spencer.

"I like dogs, though I'm more of a cat person."

"A cat person? Huh. That's interesting," Spencer said with a pointed look at Emma.

Jack couldn't quite make out what the look meant,

but Emma rolled her eyes. "You can stop."

"Oh, I'm not doing anything."

"Hey Spence," a woman said with a quick kiss on Spencer's cheek. "Hey Em." She pulled Emma in for a hug. "I didn't expect to see you until this weekend."

The woman was short, just over five feet, with black shoulder length hair and brown skin.

"Yeah, I'm just showing my... Jack around. Jack, this is Clare, Spencer's ma... girlfriend."

Clare waved. "Nice to meet you." She turned to Emma. "Did he tell you we just checked out the new venue down here? We're officially playing a gig there next month."

"Oh, yeah." Emma gave her a high five. "I'll be there."

"Jack here hates dogs," Spencer said to Clare as he wrapped his arm around her waist and pulled her close.

"I don't hate dogs. I just prefer cats." Jack frowned at her brother. No one ever judged him based on his preference for cats. Could this question make or break the budding relationship between Emma and him? Did he even want to have a long-term relationship? When she said she'd be at the gig next month, his stomach dropped. She'd be here, and he'd be home. Over three hundred miles away.

Clare shook her head at her boyfriend, then turned to Jack. "Do you like big dogs or small dogs better?"

"If I have to choose, I'd go for a small dog. One that will fit in my lap. You know, like a cat." Jack winked at Emma and waited for Spencer's reaction.

Spencer didn't disappoint. His eyes grew big, and his

mouth dropped open in mock hurt. His hand thumped his chest. "Say it ain't so! Small dogs? Emma, I don't approve of him."

Emma smiled and pushed his forehead back. "What exactly do you think you're not approving of? You know what? Don't answer that. I don't need your approval." She grabbed Jack's hand and pulled him away. "Bye you two," she said with a wave.

"Bye," Clare called. "Are you coming over Saturday morning?"

"I'll come on Sunday, if that's okay."

"That's fine. See you Sunday."

As they walked away, Spencer stood beside Clare hunched over, pouting down at his other half, who laughed before pulling him into a kiss.

Jack dutifully followed Emma. "I like them. They're cute together."

"They're cuter when I don't hear them banging. He lives in our childhood home, and it didn't take me long to learn to knock before entering."

"You could always put in earplugs."

"Well, it's his house. I'd rather not risk walking in on him having sex." Her face scrunched up. "Gross."

He chuckled. "I understand. I've walked in on my sister and it's scarring." He shivered.

With just one movement, he could have his arm around Emma's waist, pulling her close enough to smell her hair and kiss her. How would he be able to leave once he found Pablo? For now, he just basked in the moment and followed her to dinner.

Chapter 5

Jack

Friday morning found Jack in his car following his tracker through Savannah. Paul flew down and didn't understand Jack's insistence on driving. The need to get around in his search for Pablo outweighed the comfort of flying. The trip may very well take him further away from Savannah after they completed the hotel business. Not all the hotel's employees were privy to the other side of the company.

The coin sized disc in Jack's hand showed a glowing green line that pointed in the direction of the person who's being tracked. Rather, Frank, the seer who cracked the code on how to locate Pablo, created it to track one specific person. Jack didn't quite understand all of it, only that it tracked Pablo's brain, not his body. With a tracking distance of only ten miles, it narrowed down Jack's ability to find him.

The glowing green light led him to the Georgia Southern of Savannah campus. It made sense. Pablo looked college aged.

He parked in the visitor parking and walked around with the tracker hidden in the palm of his hand leading the way. Students began filing out of buildings, walking across the campus as he approached.

Class change. He groaned. It would be easier if Pablo stayed put. The tracker would fluctuate directions and if he's close to the target, those fluctuations became dramatic.

Just as he predicted, the pointer swung to the right. Jack picked up the pace, dodging students.

He turned left, following the tracker's needle, running into a young man, knocking his books on the ground.

"I'm so sorry," Jack said, and he scooped down to pick up the books as fast as possible. Once the guy was settled, Jack broke out into a run. He came across a parking lot, and he slowed to check the tracker. It once again swung right. When Jack looked up, a man with long black hair driving away caught his attention. He squinted and recognized Pablo. The car turned toward the exit of campus as Jack tried to race after it.

"Shit," he yelled. The tracker dug into his hand as he clenched his fist around it. From this distance, he wouldn't catch him, and he couldn't even make out the plates.

He jammed the device into his pocket before he lost control and threw it. His phone dinged, letting him know he had little time before his next meeting. Was it worth ditching to find Pablo now that he'd seen him? Yes, of course. Did he want to risk his sister's wrath? No. She liked to remind him of what brought in the money to keep the Brotherhood going.

He shook his head and sighed. He'd start again Monday at the university. The walk back to his car took longer than he imagined. Just how far did he run? Once in his car, he drove off toward downtown to meet Paul. How long would this hotel business take?

~

Emma

Emma paced Ethan's office. When she called to talk to him, he told her to meet him here. His class ended soon, and he had time before the next one. She picked up a textbook from his desk that he undoubtedly taught from and flipped through it. He'd worked as a professor of biology here for a long time, before it became Georgia Southern. She spied Armstrong memorabilia on the wall and wondered how he felt about the change in name and management. The consolidation happened a few years ago, but if he wasn't happy, he would have retired.

She made her way to the window and looked down from his third-floor window and noticed students coming out of buildings. Class change. He'd be here soon. The students made their way between buildings, waving at people they knew or stopping to talk.

Someone came into view, walking faster than the

others. Recognition shot through her. Jack. What was he doing there? Maybe it's not Jack. She only got a rear side look, but the resemblance was uncanny.

"Emma, I'm glad you're here."

She jumped at her name and turned to the door. Ethan walked in and put his pile of notes on his desk.

"Did... I startle you?" He grinned and his eyes twinkled.

"Maybe." She left the window and took a seat in one of the visitors' chairs.

She picked up on his soft chuckles as he closed and locked the door.

"Serious conversation," Emma smirked. "You sure you want to have it with me?"

"Don't be silly. Of course, or I wouldn't have called you."

Ethan had a way of overlooking Emma's smartass remarks. It reminded her of her dad. Her dad and Ethan never engaged in the banter if something was serious, but Ethan rarely joked around at all.

"What's this about?" She hoped he hadn't heard about Jack. It was something she wanted to tell him. She knew Wes, Spencer, and Clare would keep it a secret, but she didn't know who else might have seen them together.

"I've been having conversations with Sylvia about our next step regarding our... hunter problem."

"Okay. I don't even know what step we are on."

"You know how Sylvia likes to keep things quiet. We've sent people to scout out the other locations of the organization. The information we had didn't explain exactly what research each facility was engaged in, but we know each facility conducts different research.

"It seems they didn't have much information on the other facilities at the one we... visited."

Visiting was an interesting way to say 'snuck into the facility, broke the bond a bad guy held with Hayley, battled hunters while trying to liberate captives who were hunters in disguise (can you say trap), then ran for their lives when the building caught on fire.' No matter how many times Ethan swept for bugs, he preferred to use vague speech.

"I don't imagine the other research facilities are any less tragic and dangerous."

"It's all very concerning, and time is limited, otherwise we might attempt to apply for a job there."

"Apply for a job? What would the listing say?" Emma thought 'Now hiring henchmen ready to battle the supernatural,' wouldn't exactly work on a job search site.

He looked at her like he might scold her. "From what Sylvia has told me, four of the five books Cernunnos needs are in their hands. Their focus will be on the coven."

"When did they get the fourth?"

"Two days ago, from what Sylvia told me."

"But they don't have the last book, right? That's what Sylvia said?"

Ethan frowned. "It is what she said, but recently, she told me we must protect Maggie at all costs."

"Like two months ago, when she was being

targeted?"

"Yesterday. She said it yesterday again."

Emma leaned forward and put her elbows on her knees. "Why Maggie and not anyone else? If she knew where the book was, she'd have told me."

"The old woman keeps secrets from everyone. Just keep what I told you in mind and don't tell anyone, not even Maggie."

"Old woman? Aren't you older than her? And I'm guessing you didn't have permission to tell me about Maggie either."

"You are exactly right. On all of it. But Sylvia feels older than me. She always seemed more responsible."

Years ago, Ethan seemed happy being second to Emma's father, Walter. He used to say he had the fun job of picking up loose ends, which meant entertaining the kids. Now, with Walter gone, Ethan stepped up to lead. Now he worked closely with his own second, Isaiah, and had tons of support from his wife.

Sylvia, however, thrived under lists of responsibilities. Chaos was most certainly her weakness.

"So, what exactly do you need me to do?" Emma cocked her head to the side. He wouldn't tell her this if he didn't need her for something.

"Just keep doing what you're doing. Maggie's your best friend. Someone close to her needs to know that she's at greater risk than she realizes. Somehow, Maggie and the book are connected, whether or not she knows it."

Emma sat back and rested her elbows on the

armrests. How could Ethan sit there and tell her not to tell Maggie? They'd been best friends for over twenty years. She took a deep breath and put herself in Ethan's shoes. He was in charge of keeping the peace with the other supernatural groups in the area, mostly with the local coven. He'd gotten a glimpse of something Sylvia, the coven leader, knew, and still opted to tell Emma. He trusted her with this knowledge, even though it could cause strife between the two leaders.

"I won't tell Maggie. For now." She stood up and stretched. "Anything else?"

"No. You?"

She studied him for a second, sitting behind the desk in a button-up shirt, gray hair peppered throughout his hair. He was the closest thing she had to a father.

"I found my mate," she told him.

"Really? That's great news. Tell me about her."

Emma laughed. "His name is Jack. And he lives in Winston-Salem."

Ethan's eyebrows scrunched together. "Winston-Salem, huh?"

"Yeah."

"Does he know about us? You?"

"No. He's human."

"I'd like to meet him when you get a chance."

"Sure. I'll see what I can do."

"I know I shouldn't say this, but..."

"Don't bite him?"

"I was going to ask you not to leave. I have no right to ask you this. And if you choose to move away, I won't stop you. But you don't know how important you are to me, to the pack. And why would you bite him?"

Emma smirked and shrugged. "Seemed like something people would tell me."

"Yeah, when you were seven." He rolled his eyes. "Get out of here."

"Good. I need my beauty sleep, especially since I'm working nights."

She waved as she walked out the door. He didn't want her to leave? Did he really consider her important to the pack? Huh.

Chapter 6

Emma

Friday night, Maggie walked into Emma's house with her hands full of weighted down canvas bags. One set of bags found their place in Emma's hands as Maggie pushed past her into the kitchen. She pulled containers of food out of the bags and placed them all over the counters.

"What's all this?" Emma peeked into one of the bags in her hands. She did not know what Maggie had planned when she called to ask if she was both home and hungry thirty minutes before.

"It's dinner. And since you obviously don't have a date tonight, you can tell me all about last night's date."

Maggie popped open a plastic container to reveal a pile of fried chicken. Emma breathed in the glorious scent. She loved her best friend's cooking.

Once all the containers were out and opened, Maggie pulled plates down from the cabinets and nudged

Emma to make a plate.

Emma sat at the kitchen table and dug into her dinner. "It tastes so good. You should be my personal chef."

"Oh yeah? I hope you like leftovers." She laughed before taking another bite.

Emma loved her time with her best friend. They'd been friends since her dad and Maggie's Gigi brought them together almost twenty years ago. Each of them encapsulated an outsider attitude. One learning magic without being a witch and the other barely half a wolf. It didn't take long for them to be attached at the hip, despite the two-year age difference.

They told each other everything and dropped anything to help the other. Emma couldn't ask for a better friend.

"So, tell me all about your date." Maggie sat back in her chair and stretched out her short legs.

"It was nice. He took me to Husk Wednesday night and then we walked around before I needed to leave. Then last night we walked around River Street."

"Ooh, Husk. Doesn't Wes work there?"

Emma's face fell. "What? How did you know that? I didn't know that until two days ago."

"Are you kidding me? That's the only thing he talked about the last time I saw him." Maggie's narrowed eyes and pursed frown made Emma shrug.

"Anyway," Maggie continued, "tell me about the guy. Jack."

Emma couldn't stop herself from smiling. "He's nice

and funny. Admirable career goals. He's easy to read and is a great kisser."

"Girl, you kissed on the first date? Stop it."

"Oh, shut it. Kissing on the first date is normal."

Maggie laughed. "Spill more. Career? Where does he live? Family? Hobbies? Shoe size?"

"You're the worst," Emma smirked at her friend. "He works for Bellamy Hotels right now but wants to be a mediator. He told me about his sister and his dad. We didn't go into hobbies too much. He lives in Winston-Salem, and I know you don't want to know his shoe size, nor would I tell you."

"You need to let me live vicariously through you."

"I'm not going to share the sex stuff. You know that."

"Wait, go back. He lives in Winston-Salem? Is that Winston-Salem, North Carolina?"

Emma said, "Yes," then stuffed a biscuit into her mouth.

"You have to stop chewing sometime. Is he going to move here? I know he's your mate, but that's hours away. That's…" She pulled out her phone and furiously poked at it. "That's five hours away. What's your plan to get him to move here?"

The thought crossed her mind several times over the last few days. Long distance wouldn't be great, but she could do it for a while. But without the bond active on his end, he may not be interested in that sort of relationship. And if she told him they were fated mates too soon, he might bail altogether. But one idea she'd considered over the last few days wouldn't sit right with her best friend.

"You know, he wouldn't automatically have to move here."

"Eventually he would. If he wanted to be with you." Maggie took a sip of her drink.

"I could move there."

Maggie choked on the liquid. Her wide eyes glared at Emma. "I'm sorry. Did you just say you wanted to move?"

Emma scratched her head. "No. I don't want to move, but it's not out of the realm of possibilities."

"You can't move. What about the pack? What about Spencer? Or fuck. What about me?"

"In this hypothetical situation that we're discussing, you could visit all the time. We would talk on the phone all the time, just like we do now. Spencer is with Clare now. They're in a bubble of constant bliss. He's a grown man and doesn't need me."

"The pack needs you."

Emma laughed. "No, they don't. The pack hasn't ever needed me. I'm not even a full wolf. I'm some genetic anomaly. I'm sure they appreciate the help I give, but nothing would change if I didn't show up each month. They don't ask for my opinion and rarely use it when I offer. And frankly, I don't need them either. I don't shift. I can stay home or go out clubbing during a full moon and nothing would happen. I'm one of two lingering connections to the last leader. With me gone, they still have Spencer."

Maggie pushed away from the table, then lunged into Emma's lap, her arms wrapped around her neck. "No. None of that matters. You can't leave. I won't let you." Maggie's face pressed against Emma's shoulder. "I'll kidnap him first. Then you can be happy right next to me, and we can continue to be exasperated with the coven and pack. Together."

Emma rubbed her friend's back, propping her chin on Maggie's head. She didn't want to leave her friend or Savannah. But the pull in her stomach that connected her to Jack was getting stronger, and they had only met two days ago. Maggie might actually kidnap him if she couldn't convince him to move to Savannah.

"No kidnapping people."

"It's only a last resort."

"Me moving away is the last resort." Emma kissed her head. "Now get off my lap. I have food to eat."

"No. If I move, you'll leave."

"You're being ridiculous." Emma's fingers found the right spot on Maggie's side and tickled her.

"Ahh. Stop." A squirming Maggie jumped out of Emma's lap. "Bad Emma."

Emma leaned back in her seat and could feel Maggie's stare. Emma rolled her eyes and stared back. "What?"

"I always thought that when you found your mate, they would be a woman."

Laughter filled the kitchen. Once Emma calmed down, she said, "Me too, girl. Me too."

"How do you feel about being stuck with cock for the rest of your life?" Maggie's lips twitched upward enough for Emma to notice.

She expected a rush of disappointment when she

thought about the question. Emma never limited her partners to one gender, though she enjoyed her times with women more than with men. Feelings of discontent never came. Instead, a sense of acceptance washed over her.

"I don't know. Here's hoping he knows how to use his dick." She smirked at her friend, who could no longer hide her grin.

"I'll buy you a new toy, just in case."

Emma laughed. Knowing Maggie, she'd send the most misshapen toy she could find.

"I took him to River Street last night and ran into Spencer and Clare."

"Really?" Maggie scooted back into her seat. "What did they think?"

"Spencer asked him if he liked dogs or cats more."

Maggie grinned. "What did he say?"

Emma rolled her eyes. "Cats."

"No! That's hilarious."

Emma agreed only because she liked cats more as well, but they didn't seem to like her back. She gave her last cat to Pablo and Hayley because the cat liked them more. Maybe she could get another cat with Jack.

"Now Spencer thinks there's something wrong with him."

"Obviously. Did you tell Spencer that Jack's your mate?"

"No. It's not his business at the moment. I also don't want him running his mouth."

"Yeah. That can be a problem. You tell him and then

he tells Keon and Keon is the real gossip." Maggie stood and grabbed a small square container and two spoons, then sat down at the table.

Emma peeled off the top. "Oh, dessert."

She grabbed a spoon from Maggie and scooped out some of the bread pudding. It melted in her mouth, and she moaned.

"Will you moan like that when he feeds you some of his special cream?" Maggie snickered.

"I hate you," Emma laughed.

Chapter 7

Emma

Saturday morning, Emma leaned against a pillar outside of Jack's hotel with a list of places to visit. Thank the gods it was October and not August. Savannah stayed warm even in the fall, but nothing like the sticky, humid heat of summer.

The automatic doors on the front of the building opened and Jack walked out. His well-worn jeans hung on his hips. A half tucked in gray t-shirt stretched across his chest. The button-down shirts he wore hid his toned body. She would have a harder time reining in her libido and her wolf today. The sounds of panting already echoed in her head.

His smile widened when he saw her, and he wrapped her in a hug.

"Hey," he said and kissed her cheek.

"Hey." She reluctantly pulled away from the hug

after inhaling his scent but kept her hands on his upper arms. "Are you ready for what I have in store for you?"

"Yes. I think. Where are you taking me?" She placed her hand in the crook of his arm and walked to the sidewalk.

"I'm taking you on a journey of discovery." She waved her free hand in front of them. "Discovery of the best coffee in the city."

His eyes lit up. "Really? That's great. Where are we going first?"

"We're headed north from here to a few boutique coffee shops, then we'll swing around to hit Savannah Coffee Roasters. After that, we'll hop in my car and travel further south past Forsyth Park to The Sentient Bean and other shops in that direction. I recommend drinking water between each shop. We're going to try a lot of coffee today."

"How many places are we going to try, exactly?"

"At least eight. But I can support more."

"Should we do this like wine tasting? Sip, swish, spit?"

"Gross. But it might be better for our hearts. Just don't spit on the floor."

"Ruin my fun, why don't you?"

Emma laughed and led him down the street, deeper into downtown. By the second cup, she began holding his hand as they walked through the streets. After the third cup, they both only took sips.

"I still can't believe you're trying each of these black. Not even a bit of creamer," Emma said as she sipped on the third cup. "Some of the stronger coffee around here is too bitter to taste the differences without something to cut it."

Jack lifted the coffee, then stuck out his pinky and took a sip. "I am, what you could call, a coffee snob," he said in a terrible British accent.

~

Jack

The vibrations running through Jack's veins were mostly because of the coffee, especially since he drank two cups before meeting Emma, but he couldn't deny that his proximity to her increased them. Her smile wiped away the reason for his visit. Her touch, which became constant by the second cup, melted away any concerns he had about pursuing an actual relationship with her. Jack knew he was in trouble, but he couldn't find it in him to care.

She pointed out shops she liked along the walk. Told stories of her adventures growing up here. He listened to the tale of her first pub crawl where she and her friend Maggie ended up singing karaoke, having abandoned the crawl halfway through. It took the rest of their friends about an hour to find them. They found Emma and Maggie on stage, wearing only their bras. Emma laughed at his expression. She told him it was hot, and they were drunk, so it seemed like a good idea, especially when you get drunk in your early twenties.

He shared his own embarrassing stories. He told tales

of his sister and him playing hide and seek in his family's fancy hotels. They used to get caught by the guests. Once they snuck out all the kids from a wedding reception, none of which they knew, and convinced them to play as well. Neither of them was allowed to visit any of the hotels for years after it took the adults two hours to find them. They'd ended up in an empty room, all passed out on the floor.

Before he knew it, he started regaling her with tales of camping with his best friend, Dakota. How they would race to the river and would try to find short cuts straight up a mountain instead of taking the switchback trail. He left off the part where Dakota led the way in his wolf skin.

Stories of Dakota spilled out of him. Going to school together, being each other's wingmen, and more.

"When Dakota started working as an event coordinator at a competing hotel, we didn't talk as much. Not because of the hotel, just due to how busy he became. We stopped talking once a day and set up a time to meet once a week." Jack frowned, his mind back to his purpose in Savannah.

He stared off over the sidewalk they were walking. The tree limbs hung over the walkway and swayed in the wind. His mind went back to his last conversation with Dakota. He'd called and told Jack he couldn't meet that week. He had a date. At the time, Jack felt annoyed. He'd had a hard week and wanted to blow off some steam, but he wouldn't tell Dakota that. He didn't want to ruin his best friend's night. Instead of calling the next day, like he normally would after his friend's date, he put it off because he wanted to pout. Maybe if he'd called sooner.

Emma squeezed his arm. "That's nice getting together once a week at a set time. Maggie and I just sort of show up unannounced."

He nodded.

"Are you okay?" Emma asked. "You look lost in thought and a little sad."

He kissed her cheek. "I'm okay. Let's keep going."

She pulled him along as she gave him the side eye. He didn't want to spill his guts. They'd only known each other for a few days. As much as he knew he needed to look for Pablo for answers, he couldn't walk away from Emma.

He watched her while they walked down the street. He'd have to leave as soon as he got a new lead. How would he feel about her after a few weeks apart? Promising to come back to her wasn't in the cards. Yet, even thinking that made his heart ache.

"Okay," Emma said when she stopped in front of another coffee shop. "Two more shops and we'll hop in a car and travel south. Before I drink anything else, I need a pee break. I'll be right back." She pushed through the door and traveled toward the back of the shop to the restroom.

He pulled out his phone and took notes about the last cup of coffee. The competition for the best coffee in Savannah was steep. Any of the places Emma took him to today would be a great addition to the newest Bellamy Hotel.

He shoved his phone back in his pocket and watched

the people walking by. One person caught his eye. He'd recognize that walk anywhere, even if the longer hair would take getting used to.

Before he could stop himself, he called out, "Pablo."

His old roommate stopped and looked around. When his eyes met Jack's, he took off. Jack didn't think twice and chased after him. It didn't take long for Jack to lose track of the werewolf, but he didn't give up. The small, coin-sized tracking device was in his pocket. He pulled it out and started following the direction of the needle at a run.

After navigating six blocks, he caught sight of Pablo. Jack tried to soften the sounds of his run, but Pablo turned and took off again. Damn werewolf's ears. Two more blocks and a sharp left turn landed Jack on his ass, and pain radiated from his left eye. Pablo stood above him.

"I don't know what you want, but I'm not going back."

"What?" Jack held his eye and tried to roll to his feet. "I just want to talk."

Pablo pushed him back down with his boot. "I don't believe you."

He looked him up and down with his right eye. Pablo visibly shook, his hands curled into fists, and if looks could kill, Jack would be laid out on the sidewalk.

Pablo moved his foot and took one step back. "I don't want anything to do with you or your organization."

Jack frowned and attempted to stand again. A foot to his stomach and another punch to his face kept him down. He looked down to see drops of blood pool under his chin. The pain in his stomach didn't lessen when he wrapped his arms around it. Fuck. He needed to follow Pablo.

Using the fence nearby, he pulled himself to his feet. Pablo was gone and the needle on the tracker had faded. He probably hopped into a car and took off. It would take him hours to find him again, but only if he stayed in the city. Either way, he needed to head back to the hotel and grab a healing potion. Attending meetings with city officials sporting a black eye didn't sound like a good idea. It would take twenty-four hours for him to fully heal with the potion, but he could still grab the car and try to find Pablo again.

The pain in his stomach and face throbbed as he turned around to head to the hotel, only he didn't know where he was. Thank the gods for smartphones. He pulled it out and noticed a missed call and a few text messages. All from Emma.

Dread washed over him. Emma. Fuck. He'd forgotten all about her when he saw Pablo. With no idea what to tell her, he stalled while he pulled up the GPS map on his phone.

He walked north with a slight hobble as he thought about Emma and Pablo. If only he could tell Emma everything. The sigh that left him sounded more like a moan. At the next crosswalk, he leaned against the building and sent a text to Emma.

"I'll call you tomorrow," he typed, then deleted the entire message. He moaned as the pain hit him again. The blinking cursor in the message block mocked him. What could he tell her? Lying didn't sound like a good idea, but it didn't sound terrible either.

"I'm so sorry I left," he began. "I got a call from Paul and had to go bail him out of jail. Something about being drunk. I'll call you later."

The heart emoji stared at him. It seemed like too much, but it might work. He sighed and added it. With the lie he was sending, adding a heart wouldn't hurt either way. He pressed the send button and gathered his energy to push himself off the building and shuffled the rest of the way to the hotel. As he entered his room, he knew he wasn't leaving it until the next day. He needed that potion and some rest.

Chapter 8

What the ever-loving fuck? Did her fated mate just ditch her?

Emma paced in front of the coffee shop and checked her phone again. No response after the texts she'd sent. She felt a growl rumble in her chest. After all these years of hearing stories of fated mate bonds and she'd never heard of the non-shifter taking off. Of course, it would happen to the carrier.

Real wolf, my ass, she thought.

Her foot tapped on the ground, and she ground her teeth as she called Jack. The last time she was close to this mad, she killed someone. After that realization, she forced herself to relax, letting out the breath she'd been holding.

She breathed through her nose. Her sense of smell wasn't bad for a wolf. No one had as good a sense of smell as Spencer, but she'd categorize herself as better than average. After a few steps, she caught his scent.

Why did he cross the street? She rolled her eyes and followed her nose. The path twisted and turned throughout the city and through a square. His scent began to peter out. Too many people walked through here. The bus exhaust from all the tour buses exacerbated the problem, and halfway through the square she'd lost him and her olfactory abilities. Between the exhaust and the woman who passed wearing enough perfume to cover a dead body, Emma's nose stopped working.

The vibration of her phone startled her.

"I'm so sorry I left. I got a call from Paul and had to go bail him out of jail. Something about being drunk. I'll call you later. 🖤 "

The text glared at her, and she glared right back. Jail? She didn't think so. Didn't he know arrest records are public information? It gave him at least a day before she could check the arrest records. When exactly were Jesi and Chuck coming home, anyway?

With a sigh, she turned and stormed her way to her car. Heart emoji. What did he think he'd accomplish with a heart emoji? He didn't feel the mate pull that bastard. No one played Emma Luvel. Not even her mate.

She slammed her car door and pulled out into traffic, but the fire in her started to die down. What if he'd told the truth? He could have waited five minutes to let her know. When she parked south of Forsyth Park, she wasn't sure exactly what to feel or do.

She had not figured out anything by the time she pulled open the door to Herbs and Healing, Maggie's metaphysical shop. They sold specialty teas and gifts to tourists and locals, but now, Maggie made the bulk of her sales online. The bell clanged on the door and the bright color that normally lifted her spirits pissed her off. Even the soft feel of magic on her skin annoyed her. She could do without all the shelves of rocks, herbs, and incense. At least the path to the counter was clear.

"Are you trying to burn down the shop with your eyes?" Maggie raised an eyebrow.

"What?" Emma leaned on the counter. "No."

"Where is all this attitude coming from?"

"I'm full of attitude. You don't need to comment on it."

"I do when you look like you want to watch the world burn." Maggie walked toward her workshop. "Want some tea?"

"I guess." Emma slunk around behind the counter and laid on the floor out of eyesight of any customers.

Maggie came out with two mugs and looked down. "So, the coffee date didn't go well?"

"I thought it was going great. Then I came back from the bathroom, and he'd left."

"Like disappeared or took off?"

Emma moved around to lean against the wall. "Both. I tried to track him but lost him in a high traffic area. This is the text he sent."

Emma handed her phone over to her best friend. Maggie read the text with a frown.

"Who is Paul and why is Jack bailing him out of jail?"

"Paul is his co-worker, the one trying to get a hotel built in downtown."

"It's Saturday. I would have left him there."

Emma laughed. "Yeah. But would you have left me there?"

"That's different," Maggie said, rolling her eyes. "You're my bestie. I'd stab someone in the throat for you."

"I know you can't know if someone is lying over text, but it feels like a lie."

"What's with the heart emoji? I know you might be feeling all 'heart emoji,' but he wouldn't know that. Unless you told him."

"No. I didn't tell him." Emma crossed her arms over her chest. "I was planning on telling him tonight. Now I'm second guessing everything. I wanted to at least get a blow job out of it. That was the plan. Go to my house, make out, a little oral, then 'guess what? I'm a werewolf.'"

"At least you have your priorities in order. Cunnilingus, then the heavy stuff."

Emma threw her head back and whined. "I just want to pout. My fated mate ditched me, probably lied to me, and I'm actually considering forgiving him already."

Maggie slid down the wall beside her. She pulled Emma's head down to her shoulder. "You can forgive him, and I'll punch him in the throat. Deal?"

Emma's shoulders shook with laughter. "Deal."

~

Emma

Sunday morning rolled around with Emma stuck in bed. Spencer had already sent a text asking when she was coming over. She frowned at her phone. Stupid antidote. The antidote for a werewolf's bite called for a key ingredient. The key ingredient only Emma had. The blood of a carrier.

Asymptomatic werewolf carrier. She thought about what that meant. Usually when a werewolf and a human couple have a child, they are born either a werewolf or a human. Carrier's were rare. Most werewolves only read about them. A carrier was the offspring of a werewolf and a human who could not shift but had the ability turn a human into a werewolf with a bite. They had better hearing, smell, and strength than a human. If they were bitten by a werewolf it would not make them shift. She had the scars to prove it. Little wolf's teeth marks on her thigh where Spencer played too hard as a kid. He always bit her in the same spot, causing the skin to eventually scar even with her werewolf healing ability. Punk.

Once a week, for almost three months, Spencer drew as much blood as he could to keep a steady supply of the antidote. One reason Spencer became a phlebotomist was to draw blood from Emma for the antidote. They couldn't tell if the hunters were playing with them or recruiting but packs all over the southeast were seeing an influx of werewolf bites. The supply dwindled as quickly as Maggie could make it. That meant weekly blood draws and a close eye on her diet.

Emma drove down Spencer's dirt driveway to their childhood home, to reach the house nestled in the trees. The brick house felt like home, but she didn't want to live here anymore. Her brother was more than welcome to keep the house and the land.

She looked past the house through the trees where the enclosure stood while she walked to the house. She couldn't see the enclosure from here, but that might be the safest place she ever felt. Inside the twenty-foot-tall fence during the full moons. It kept the pack safe. It kept her safe, even though she didn't need to be there.

A few cars dotted the driveway, including Maggie's. Maggie usually worked with Pablo and Hayley on Sundays. She still hadn't found what caused Pablo to shift at will after he finally escaped Cernunnos. Those bitten and turned into werewolves normally could only shift during the full moons. Those born werewolves could shift anytime. They could even keep from shifting during the full moons.

Pablo's situation intrigued them all. He left after becoming a werewolf, only to end up in the clutches of hunters, specifically Cernunnos. They experimented on him for months before he escaped. Now he could shift whenever he wanted, and they all wanted to know how. Pablo's mate, and fellow werewolf Hayley, offered to be Maggie's guinea pig.

Normally, she could hear them working in the backyard, but she couldn't hear them today. Clare opened the door before she could knock and gave her a hug. She pulled back and gave Emma a big smile.

"So, tell me all about him." Clare tugged on her arm.

"Ugh. I forgot you met him." Emma rolled her eyes. "I don't want to talk about him."

"What did he do?" Clare asked. "Give me five minutes, and I can be ready to bury a body."

Emma laughed. "Spencer is a terrible influence on you."

She shrugged. "Nah, I think that's Tick."

Clare led the way to the kitchen, where Spencer had all the equipment set up.

The kitchen held tons of memories of watching her father cook for the entire pack before a full moon shift. He believed that having a full stomach to start a full moon cut down on aggression once in wolf form. She never paid attention to the cooking but listened to him talk about the pack, the responsibilities he had as the pack leader, and any new projects he wanted to start.

Emma never really learned to cook, but Spencer did. After their father passed away, Spencer would cook for the two of them. Ethan picked up cooking pack dinners, but eventually those who could cook began rotating the responsibility.

A small kitchen table sat to the right of the kitchen, where they had family dinners. They reserved the dining room for when the entire pack arrived for meals. Of course, they all spilled out into the hall and into the living room and, on good days, into the backyard.

"You finally got a new table," Emma said, running her

hands over the top. "I like the different colored planks."

White, tan, and dark brown wood planks made up the tabletop. She didn't know if it was made of different wood, or if the creator stained the planks. The table legs were painted white. Three of the chairs were black and the other three were white.

"I really like it." Clare grinned up at Emma, then pulled Spencer into a hug.

"Good. I'm glad my contribution wasn't wasted on something terrible."

"You only contributed because you broke the other one." Spencer pulled out a chair and motioned for Emma to sit.

"So, mean." Emma pouted. "It was Clare's fault."

A few months ago, after Clare joined Spencer's band, they learned that Clare's voice called to their wolves when singing "Least of My Kind," a folk song written by Catherine Faber. When the wolves of the pack heard the song, it forced them to shift into their wolf skin, even those turned, not born as a wolf. With the weekly blood draws, Emma would lose energy, but if Clare sang that song to her, it triggered her inner wolf's healing power. She just couldn't hold on to anything, such as a table, or she'd break a chunk off.

"Maggie's fault. It was her idea," Clare chimed in.

Spencer checked Emma's pulse, then worked on the tourniquet on her arm. "We framed that piece of wood, by the way. We put it in the living room."

She glared at him. "Did you at least list me as the artist?"

"Of course." He put on gloves and cleaned her arm with an alcohol swab. "Before I stick you, I won't be able to draw as much as normal. Your iron isn't as strong as usual."

"Could it have something to do with Mr. Cat Lover?" Clare waggled her eyebrows. "What's his name again? Jack?"

"It's probably because I worked nights this week."

"Nope. I don't buy it." Spencer started filling up vials from the holder. "I heard about the coffee date. And you know that coffee decreases iron absorption."

"Why would I know that?" She kept a blank expression on her face, knowing she wouldn't win this argument.

Spencer tilted his head to the side and raised an eyebrow. She called it his 'are you shitting me' face, and he looked just like their father when he did it. "You're a veterinarian, and I gave you a list of iron-rich foods and a list of foods that reduce iron absorption. Coffee is on the list."

"I treat animals and animals don't consume coffee. Unless you count yourself."

The edge of his lips twitched. "Hum. No worries. Just don't drink so much coffee this week." He pulled out a needle and wrapped up her arm with a purple cohesive bandage.

"What happened to the green?" Emma preferred the green to the other colors.

"I'm out of green. You'll live with purple."

She narrowed her eyes. "You're planning

something."

Wide eyes stared back at her, and he gasped. "Me? I can't believe you would say that. I would never."

"I agree with Emma," Clare said. "You're planning something. Your eyes are doing that thing."

"Rude." He packed up his supplies and kissed Clare's forehead. He turned his head toward the hall and yelled, "Maggie, come get your secret ingredient."

Clare picked up Emma's hand and sang softly to her. Just like always, the song kickstarted her healing. If Emma were a full werewolf, she wouldn't need the song. Sometimes she thought the wolf inside her was just a lazy asshole.

Maggie sauntered in with Pablo and Hayley behind her. The pink pixie cut Maggie wore stuck up in multiple places. She liked to sit with her back on the seat, her legs over the chair or couch back, and her head hanging down.

"Lookie, Lookie. The blood of my enemies." Maggie picked up the vials, then raised an eyebrow at me. "Not get enough iron this week?"

"I've already been called out." She stretched her arms over her head. "Why are y'all inside today?"

"Pablo ran into someone yesterday. Someone from the Brotherhood that he met in North Carolina. Ethan asked if I could help."

"Is that what the meeting is about tonight?" Spencer sat next to Clare and wrapped his arm around her shoulders.

"Probably." Pablo leaned against the kitchen island with his hands in his pockets. Hayley, his mate, threaded her fingers through his long dark hair. Once upon a time, he kept his hair short, but after being captured by Cernunnos, he kept it long to hide the scars on his scalp.

"I thought you said that the Brotherhood were good," Emma said.

Pablo sighed. "I did at first, but I just don't know. I can't help thinking, 'What if they set me up? What if it was all planned?' The guy I saw yesterday… He's the one who suggested Columbia and to meet up with Rod from the local pack. When I met him, he had me in a cage within days."

"What's his name? The guy you saw yesterday?" Clare asked.

He squirmed on the spot and pulled Hayley close. "I don't remember. There's a lot that I don't remember between when I left here and when I escaped. The few names I remember are the ones who tortured me."

"I thought his name was Rodrick, not Rod," Emma said. "Rodrick Kahn."

"It is." Pablo looked down. "I can't risk it. When he called my name, I ran, and he chased me."

"I pointed out that he's probably not here for him. Savannah is a big tourist destination. He's probably here on vacation or on business." Maggie started tapping her fingers on the table. "Pablo now has a small pouch of magical blindness powder. Just hit him in the face with the pouch, and he won't be able to see for a good five minutes, plus an invisibility potion that'll last about ten minutes. There's plenty of time to get away or you could grab his wallet and get away."

"Are you starting a pick-pocket ring?" Emma raised an eyebrow. "How come I'm not invited?"

"It's so we can identify him." Hayley laughed.

"Now," Emma started, "if he takes this invisibility potion, will we still be able to see his clothes? Clothing walking around on its own tends to draw attention."

"Yes." Maggie's eyes lit up. "Just kidding, no. Anything touching his skin will also become invisible."

"So, if he's wearing socks…"

"Good point." Maggie turned to Pablo. "Maybe wear shoes that don't need socks for a week or two. Just in case you need to use the potion."

"Am I just a coward if I run again? Vanish and take off. Not very brave." Pablo looked over Hayley's head, avoiding eye contact.

"Absolutely not," Spencer answered. "We don't know what he's capable of. It's better to regroup. We don't fight unless we're prepared or cornered. Hell, I jumped into the Ohio River running from Cernunnos."

"You did what?" Clare stared at Spencer, her mouth slightly ajar.

Everyone else glanced at each other, then burst out laughing. They all settled in as Spencer told Clare about leaping off the Purple People Bridge as he lured the men tracking Pablo away from Savannah.

Chapter 9

Jack

Sunday brought less pain in Jack's head, but more to his side. He looked down and could still see bruising, even after the healing potion. Pain radiated down his side with every breath. How on earth did he stay asleep?

After a painful and slow shower, he rummaged through the bag of magic Zuri and Regina packed him. Zuri, the pack's head witch, focused on items to repair the tracking disc while Regina, his father's administrative assistant, added a magical first aid kit.

He pulled a large white rectangle of fabric from the first aid kit and read the instructions. After mixing all the herbs he needed for the spell, he pulled out his standard spell casting kit and placed the candles, crystals, and bowl of water around him. As a human, he couldn't cast a spell without it. Zuri liked to remind him that he wouldn't need to cast a circle if he practiced more. "Words, herbs, and a crystal are more than enough for your average human.”

The only spells Jack ever pulled off without casting a circle included scent blocking and step of stealth. He didn't normally have much use for other magic other than healing potions.

With all the supplies laid out on a hotel table, he lit the candles, hoped this would work without putting everything on the ground, and let the energy rise around him. Once he wrapped the fabric over his naked chest and rubbed in the herb mixture, he said,

"Record the bones inside
Impose the image to see
The strength, the structure, the breaks, the size
Show the truth, I decree."

The cloth glowed, signaling Jack to hold still. He held his breath until the glimmer died. He held up the sheet and sighed, then blew the candles out. With the sheet laid out in front of him, he could see the magical x-ray of his upper body.

He took a picture and texted it to the Brotherhood's resident doctor and asked, “Am I seeing this right?”

Two minutes later, Dr. Portsmith replied, “Yes. That is a fractured rib. What on earth happened?”

“A foot happened. I took a healing potion yesterday.” Jack slowly sat down.

“If you took a potion yesterday, you probably broke it and the potion is doing its job. Wait the full twenty-four hours and take another x-ray. If it's still there, take another potion. Either way, expect to be sore for at least another day."

"Thanks, Doc." Jack stared at the phone. He itched to call Emma. He owed her an explanation, but it wasn't one he could give. Not yet at least. How would she react to all he'd seen and everyone he knew?

The thought of ghosting her crossed his mind. Since he'd met her, she'd stayed on his mind. It wasn't like him to have someone on his mind all the time. But that smirk and her laugh popped into his head every day. He wanted to go see her, but his eye still held a bit of bruising, and anyone would notice how careful he carried himself at the moment.

He pulled out the tracker. A single dot blinked in the middle. Pablo must be out of the ten-mile range. Tracking Pablo down now didn't sound like such a good idea anyway. He couldn't run, much less walk at a normal pace.

The only other thing he wanted to do at the moment was talk to Emma. The phone burned in his hand, then rang. A smile crossed his face.

"Hey Morgan."

"How's my lil' brother?" His sister Morgan practically cooed at him over the line.

"I was happy you called until I heard your voice. Thank God you aren't right beside me. My cheeks wouldn't survive your pinching."

Her laughter over the line made him smile. "I'm calling to see how things are going. I mean, with you. Paul updated me on the hotel business."

"I bet he has. 'Ms. Morgan, I'm sending you a list of the top contractors in Savannah. Ms. Morgan, the council committee members were very agreeable to our proposals.'"

"He's not that bad. And he's married." Jack could almost hear her eyes roll while she talked. "I do make him nervous though."

"You have a big presence. Bigger than Dad's."

"Now you're trying to distract me. How are your plans coming along? I know Dad won't call, but I'm nosey. Have you found that guy yet?"

"Pablo? I found him and then he punched me in the face and kicked me while I was down."

"Ah, so that's who kicked you."

"Talking to the doc, I see."

"Of course. Too bad he can't tell when I'm flirting. He's the one I'm worried about shaking in his boots… unless we're knocking boots."

He frowned. "Gross. I don't want to think about the specifics of that. Moving on, no, I didn't talk to him. I have no idea what happened or why he ran from me."

"You've been there for almost a week, and you just found him yesterday? I think you're losing your touch."

She wasn't wrong. Jack knew exactly why it had taken him so long. "Covering for you has delayed me from working at one hundred percent."

"Oh? Does covering for me include dates with a tall brunette with an ample derriere?"

"Paul." He gritted his teeth. "It's like everyone is spying on me."

"Did you just growl?" Morgan laughed. "You must really like her. What's her name?"

Jack sighed, then settled back against the headboard. "Her name is Emma, and she's wonderful."

"Wonderful?" He could hear the shock in her voice. "Who are you, and where is my brother?"

"Stop. I like her. She's a veterinarian, gorgeous, and she delights in teasing me."

"Sounds like we'll get along. Does she know who you are?"

"Which do you mean? A Bellamy or a hunter?"

"Both."

"I told her I was a Bellamy, and she was shocked when she put it together, though she seemed more impressed with you than me. When I told her I wanted to be a mediator, she was supportive."

"I mean, you are a mediator, only between humans and supernatural beings."

"It's getting harder to convince them to trust me," he said with a sigh. "We were making great headway until a few years ago."

"I know, and you think it's connected to the disappearances of the various were-creatures. You've told me."

"And I'll keep telling you. Something big is coming. I can feel it and for once in my life, I think I'm in the right place to help."

"I know you're working hard to find Dakota. I'm worried too. But I do question the feeling you have about being in Savannah. Are you sure it's not because of Ms. Emma the wonderful?"

"Tease all you want, but she's only part of it. I know there are supernatural groups in this city, but I can't find them. Even my contacts refused to connect me with them."

"Really? That's unusual. The Brotherhood has worked hard over the last fifty years to prove ourselves trustworthy."

"Exactly. Whenever I asked, they told me it was too dangerous for me to know. Whatever is happening, the supernaturals in this city are involved."

"You never told me any of this."

"You were too busy handing me a box of paperwork and giving me information about how to help Paul."

Morgan made her short 'I'm sorry' noise. "Jack. I'm so sorry about that. Being CEO is more work than I realized."

"But you're good at it and it shows."

"Let me put out some feelers on my end. See if anyone will talk to me about Savannah. In the meantime, try to fall deeply in love. I need a good hotel manager in Savannah. Okay. Love you. Bye."

She hung up the phone before he could answer. He really loved his sister, but she tended to bulldoze him. The phone sat warm in his hand from the call. Was he falling in love? He didn't know. He was fond of Emma; she'd hadn't been far from his mind since they met. How would their relationship progress when he left? His chest tightened. Leaving sounded terrible, but he couldn't stay, even if Morgan offered him a manager's job. He'd hate it. The Brotherhood gave him purpose and the ability to help everyone. Could he do that from Savannah?

Before he could think too hard about his long-term plans, he picked up his phone to make a plan to apologize to Emma.

Chapter 10

As soon as Emma walked into the exam room, her patient, a large long-haired lab, scurried up to her and sat down, leaning on her leg. The dog gazed up at Emma, tongue hanging out, waiting to be petted. She stooped down and ran her hand through the dog's fur.

"I see Goldie is doing well today," Emma said to Mr. Brooks. She then looked down and used a softer voice for Goldie. "I'm so glad you're doing well. Especially after that chocolate fiasco two months ago."

Goldie licked Emma's face, making her laugh.

"She's doing well, and we relocated the chocolate stash. Surprisingly, she's only here for her yearly check-up." Mr. Brooks smiled at Emma. He loved Goldie and spoiled her rotten. "She's still keeping me young, even with all the trouble she gets into."

Mr. Brooks was an older gentleman, and he adopted

Goldie five years ago, but Goldie had a way of getting into trouble. She came in with staples in her foot, cat scratches on her face, and more, the most recent being her generous intake of chocolate.

"Let's take a look at her." Emma looked at the notes from the vet techs and performed her own exam. After a bit, she sent Mr. Brooks and Goldie on their way after the tech returned with her shots.

Emma loved working at the Flours Animal Hospital. Dr. Luna had a way with the animals. Emma suspected she might be part Fae, but she probably didn't know. The hospital supported the local emergency vet as well, each vet working the night shift one week per quarter. She couldn't ask for a better boss than Dr. Luna Flours.

She walked into the back, making notes on Goldie's chart before picking up the next one.

"Dr. Emma," Thomas the receptionist said. "You have a delivery. I put it in your office."

"What kind of delivery?" Emma's eyes widened and looked around. All the techs were trying to cover smiles.

"Flowers," Thomas said, dragging it out in a sing-song voice.

She raised an eyebrow at him, but he just winked and went back to the front. Emma peeked into the office and saw a vase full of pink and white flowers surrounding a single lavender rose. She didn't need to look at the card to know who it was from. She just knew.

Jack's handwriting sketched her name on the envelope. On the inside it said, "I'm sorry. Please have dinner with me tonight."

The logo at the bottom of the card was one she recognized. Genevieve, a member of the Midnight Oak Coven, owned that flower shop.

"Who is it from?" Thomas asked.

"Don't you have work to do?" Emma asked, turning and giving him her 'get back to work' look.

"Yep." He disappeared from the doorway, and she slid the note into her pants pocket. A smile crept up on her face, even though she didn't want it to. He'd ditched her on their third date, and she just forgave him with the gift of flowers. Stupid fated mates.

She snapped a picture of the flowers and sent them to Maggie.

"Hey," Emma texted. "Do these flowers have a special meaning?"

She didn't have to wait long to get a reply. "WHO SENT THE FLOWERS? DID JACK SEND THE FLOWERS?"

"Thanks for all the all caps. And yes. He apologized and wants to have dinner." Emma looked over her next patient's chart, then walked over to the exam room door just as she heard her phone chime.

"I sent the picture to Genevieve. She knows that kind of stuff. And you have to go, or you'll regret it, true love lady."

Emma rolled her eyes. "Thanks. Looks like they came from her shop," she texted back, then put away her phone, and concentrated on her work.

The flowers and Jack filled her thoughts while she worked on her patients, which included a variety of cats, dogs, birds, and even a turtle. An hour after she got the flowers, she sent Jack a message telling him 'yes' along with her address and what time he could pick her up. If he wanted to forgive her, he'd have to work for it.

Before she left for the night, Thomas poked his head into her office. "A florist didn't deliver those flowers. Just so you know."

"Who delivered them?" Emma threw her bag over her shoulder and picked up the vase.

"A very tall, handsome man with gray, mysterious eyes and the shoulders of a god."

"Shoulders of a god? I'll have to tell him that."

"Does he have a name?" Thomas followed her through the back and out the door.

"Maybe. Depends on if I forgive him or not."

"Ooh. What did he do?"

Emma frowned. "He ditched me halfway through our date on Saturday."

"Girl." He said loud enough to startle the nearby birds. "You better make him grovel at your feet."

"I plan to." She put her bag in the car and buckled up the flowers. "If there's a next time, you'll have to give me some ideas on how to make someone grovel."

"I'll send you an official operations guide." Thomas laughed and waved as he walked to his car.

Emma laughed as she drove to her house. Once there, she moved the flowers to the kitchen table, and she jumped into the shower. Just as she finished getting ready, Maggie walked into her bedroom. She regretted giving Maggie a key.

"Genevieve says she remembers this arrangement

from this morning. Said the guy wanted to send something that said 'I'm sorry.'"

"You had to drive all the way over here for that?" Emma put on the clothes she'd laid out for her date.

"Yes. He needs to know he's not messing with only you. He needs to see your support system."

Emma put on what little makeup she wore and brushed out her hair. Maggie followed her into the kitchen where the flowers sat.

"All this says I'm sorry?" She reached out and felt one of the pink flowers.

"She said what she put together is how he feels about you. He had a lot to say." Maggie pulled out her phone. "This is what the flowers mean: the pink flowers are Camellias and mean 'longing for you.' The white stuff that kind of looks like baby's breath is actually sweet woodruff and means 'humility.' The lavender rose means 'love at first sight.'"

Emma stared at the rose, and her breath caught in her throat. Lavender flower. Love at first sight. Her wolf preened inside her as if she knew it all along, but Emma's heart pounded.

"He's smooth, I'll tell you that." Maggie leaned over and smelled the arrangement. "I'll have to remember this for the next time I date."

The door rang, and Emma lifted her head. Did he really mean it? She looked over at Maggie, then went to open the door, her friend right at her heels.

Jack stood on her porch wearing a tight green shirt, jeans that hung on his hips, and a five o'clock shadow that made her want to forgive him before he spoke. Maggie pulled Emma's hair, stopping her from drooling in her doorway.

"Jack. Hi." Emma tucked her hair behind her ear. "This is my friend Maggie."

"It's nice to meet you, Maggie." He held out his hand and Maggie shook it.

"Nice to meet you as well, Jack." She pushed her way around Emma. "What are your intentions for our little girl?"

"Your little girl?" Jack's eyebrows furrowed.

Emma dropped her head in her hands. "I'm older than you."

"I intend to date her so we can get to know each other better." Jack's answer came out easily.

"Yes, yes. That's all good." Maggie leaned forward on her tiptoes. "You don't live here. How do you plan to handle this relationship when you leave?"

His eyes widened, and his mouth opened with a frown. "That's uh... That's really something I'd need to discuss with Emma."

Maggie narrowed her eyes. "How high is your pain tolerance?"

"And now it's time to go." Emma pulled her friend out of the doorway. "Lock up when you leave."

She gave Maggie a pointed look and mouthed "stop it." Her friend only grinned back at her. Jack offered his arm to Emma, and she took it, walking with him to his car.

He opened her door and heard Maggie call out from the house, "Have a howling good time. No biting. Have her home by midnight or she'll turn into a pumpkin and remember, use protection."

They settled in the car and Jack pulled out of the driveway.

"I'd apologize for her, but she's not my responsibility," Emma said.

"It's fine. I'm glad you have someone in your corner. We should all have someone like that."

She'd agreed to have dinner with Jack. How could she not? She already felt tethered to him without completing the bond, and she itched to seal it. Sleep proved hard the past two nights. The dreams about him were way beyond PG-13 and straight into X territory.

How on earth did Spencer hold himself back for more than a week with Clare? She wouldn't put it past herself to jump him at the restaurant.

She looked over at him. He looked a bit wide eyed. "You seem bewildered."

"I feel bewildered. Does she leave everyone feeling that way?"

Emma laughed. "No. Not when you get used to her. In fact, it's usually both of us that leave people feeling that way."

"I can attest to you making me feel bewildered, but not in the same way." He glanced over at her and for a split second she felt completely naked, totally seen, and she trembled.

"I know exactly how you feel."

~

Jack

Jack took her to Cotton and Rye, another suggestion from the same hotel employee. The place looked like a converted office building, but they added brown slatted walls around the front and side that gave it character.

Inside, they sat at a two-person table. It was all Jack could do not to stare at Emma. While they waited for their order to arrive, Jack covered her hand with his.

"Emma, thank you for having dinner with me. I'm sorry for leaving so suddenly on Saturday. The whole thing was a mess." He squeezed her hand. She didn't move it, which he took as a good sign.

"I have to say, I was really shocked to find you gone. You could have stayed another few minutes to let me know you needed to go."

"Honestly, I panicked. I've never had to bail someone out of jail before, and I knew my sister would be pissed if I didn't. It wasn't until I got there that my brain caught up with me." He picked up her hand and kissed it. "Please forgive me."

She cocked an eyebrow and narrowed her eyes. A frown graced her pouting lips. "I suppose I forgive you. This time."

"I'll take it." His shoulder instantly relaxed. He knew he still needed to prove his worth to her, which seemed strange since they lived so far apart, but he didn't want to walk away from this. If his feelings kept growing, he would need a plan to tell her the truth.

For the rest of the night, they laughed and ate. It felt like he'd known her forever, yet, at the same time, couldn't learn enough about her.

"We should go dancing," he said. He wanted to feel her swaying in his arms and staring into her eyes.

"I'd like that." She leaned her chin on her hand. "My brother's band has a gig this Thursday. You could come with me and dance there."

"I'd love to go with you. What kind of music do they play?"

"Punk. Alternative. They mostly play covers." She smiled at him.

He hoped that she only gave him that soft smile. The one that called to him to kiss her. "That sounds perfect." Any music would be perfect as long as he danced with her.

The night ended with him kissing her against his car this time. She snuck her cold hand under his shirt, but he didn't mind. He lost his fingers in her hair. He pulled at it slightly, and she kissed him deeper. Her body pressed against his, and he knew she could feel his growing erection. He bucked his hips, and they both moaned.

The whistle of some people passing by startled them out of their lust for each other. Who knew exactly how long they had been making out in the parking lot? She pulled back and wiped his mouth clean.

They held hands the entire drive to her house. At her door, he kissed her again against the door. He wouldn't mind kissing her all day. Before too long, she pulled back.

"Come over for dinner tomorrow." She didn't exactly ask, but he didn't mind.

"I can't. I'm having dinner with some investors or something. Paul is adamant that I attend." He frowned.

"How about Wednesday?"

"I can be here Wednesday. Any time."

She pulled him into one more slow kiss that might kill him on the spot with need, then opened her door and wished him goodnight. He floated all the way back to his hotel.

~

Emma

What was she thinking when she asked him to dinner? She couldn't cook. After Maggie laughed at her for committing to something like this, she suggested Emma order takeout.

Emma took her suggestion to order takeout and would pass it off as her own. She'd decided that tonight was the night she came clean. About the supernatural. Not her lack of cooking skills.

She picked up pork chops, a vegetable plate, and peach cobbler from Sisters of the New South. Did she feel a bit embarrassed to re-plate everything and fake dirty dishes? Absolutely. And she would never admit this to anyone, especially Maggie. She'd tease her until they died.

When Jack arrived, her nervousness only grew. She led him to the kitchen table, where she had already laid everything out. She threw the cobbler in the oven before he arrived to make everything appear more authentic.

The problem with having Jack in her home, with just the two of them, is she didn't want to talk. Or eat. She tried to keep up with the conversation, but honestly, she couldn't stop picturing him naked, laying across the table or bending her over it.

"You haven't eaten much, are you okay?" Jack asked. He'd almost eaten everything off his plate.

"Yeah. Just not so hungry tonight."

"Well, everything tastes delicious. I'm sure it will taste just as good tomorrow."

"Me too. It'll be nice to have a good meal for lunch tomorrow instead of a sandwich." Oh, she liked this man so much. She just stared at his gray eyes and at his mouth wrapped around the fork that would feel great on her clit.

"Do you smell that?" Jack shook her out of her thoughts.

"Smell what?" Emma lifted her head and sniffed. Was something burning?

"Do you have something in the oven?"

She jumped out of her seat. "The cobbler."

She pulled the slightly charred, smoking peach cobbler out of the oven. This might be worse than admitting up front she couldn't cook.

"It's ruined," she lamented as she fanned away the smoke with the potholder.

His arms wrapped around her middle. "It's okay. No worries." Jack kissed her neck. "We don't need peach cobbler."

She turned in his arms. "But now you don't have dessert."

"I can think of something I'd like for dessert."

A smile spread across her face. "Oh, yeah?"

"Of course."

He pulled her away from the oven and kissed her. It started soft and slow, but she couldn't hold back much longer. She plunged forward desperately. The heat between them skyrocketed. She sucked on his tongue just to hear his moan, which did things to her that no other noise did. All she knew was she needed something, anything, from him now.

She pulled him out of the kitchen and into her bedroom. He landed on his back on her bed, and she climbed on top, straddling his hips. She pulled off his shirt and admired his toned body. He didn't have a six-pack, but she liked a man she could cuddle.

She traced her fingers down his chest and looked at the tattoo he had on the left side of his torso. It was an old-fashioned balancing scale that looked like the scales of justice with the word 'Conlegium' written in an old English script written underneath, all surrounded by a pentagon.

Her fingers outlined the pentagon, then the scales. "What does the word mean?"

"It means fellowship, fraternity, brotherhood, or guild. The kind of unity you have between a found family."

She smiled and leaned down to kiss it. "I like it."

He peeled her shirt off and pulled her down into a

kiss. His hands roamed all over her body and into the back of her pants to grab her ass. Her hands were not any better, grabbing and rubbing all over his beautiful body. She unbuttoned his pants and slipped her hand inside. His hard cock in her hand felt thick. She bucked her hips a bit, just thinking of it sliding inside her.

Moving her mouth, she kissed and sucked all down his neck and gave him hickies all over his shoulders where no one would see them. Her hand stroked his dick, and she could feel drops of pre-cum slide on to her hand.

His hand pulled her bra up and cupped her breast. A small pinch of her nipple had her bucking again. He rolled them over and pushed her pants down. His fingers pushed under her panties and over her clit. His mouth swallowed her moan, kissing her senseless when he slipped two fingers into her core.

She pumped his cock harder, twisting just a little as he moaned. He kissed down her neck, moved his fingers in and out, and nipped at her shoulders. Her hand faltered on his erection. The more he moved in and out of her, the more he brushed against her nub. She tried to push past the pleasure and focus on the task in her hand by rubbing her thumb over the head. He shuddered above her but didn't stop.

They thrusted and bucked into each other's hands, gazing into each other's eyes until his thumb rubbed against her clit, and she knew her eyes rolled back. She exploded around his digits, and he slowed his movement, but didn't stop until her shivers did. He took his dick into his hand and pumped until he came all over her stomach with a groan of pleasure.

Normally, she didn't like the act of spewing ejaculate all over someone, but with Jack, she loved it. He claimed her in his own human way. She stopped herself from rubbing it in but dipped her finger in to taste. It surprised her how much she liked the flavor. She'd never enjoyed it before, but now she might beg to suck him off on a regular basis.

He leaned over and kissed her, his hands wrapping around the back of her neck and the other on her lower back. The strength he must have to lean over with zero arms to prop himself up on surprised her. She's never met such an impressive human.

Chapter 11

Jack

Jack walked along the river in the early afternoon the next day. The cool breeze blew over his skin, and he breathed in the water's smell. This was a place he could see himself staying.

In a few hours, he would meet Emma for their next date. She wanted to take him to see the band 'Wolves on Fire.' Her brother was the lead guitarist, and his girlfriend was the lead singer. Afraid Emma's love for her brother blinded her perception to the band's skill, he'd mentioned the band to a few people around town and everyone agreed the band sounded amazing. Jack didn't want to hurt Emma's feelings and wanted to know what to expect.

After looking up the band and listening to a few songs, he wouldn't need to worry about faking his reaction. He could only fake liking certain styles of music for so long, though he could probably suffer through anything as long as Emma danced with him.

He turned away from the river and moved across the street to the shops. He wanted to bring his sister a gift, and he wanted it to be a good one. The last of the meetings Paul scheduled ended earlier that day, so Jack had time to browse the shops.

While deciding between two books on Bonaventure Cemetery, he caught a glimpse of someone through the window. Pablo walked past, holding a large bag in his hand. Jack dropped the books and made his way out of the door. Instead of calling out to him, he followed a good ten feet behind.

Jack didn't want to corner him, but he wanted him to stop and have a conversation. He followed him off River Street and onto Bay, heading south into the heart of downtown.

Following Pablo wouldn't end well, he knew that, but needed to know if he knew anything about Dakota. So, he kept pace with the werewolf. The path became more congested as they walked until Pablo stopped abruptly. He checked his pockets, then the bags in his hand. With one look behind him, he saw Jack.

His eyes widened before he took off at a run, his search for whatever was forgotten. Jack took off after him and pulled out the tracking device three blocks over after losing sight of Pablo.

The tracker sent him down a few crowded streets before turning into an empty alley. He skidded to a stop to find Pablo taking a swig of something.

"Pablo, I need to talk to you."

"No." Pablo's voice sounded hard and cold, then he disappeared in front of Jack.

His body faded, starting with his head, and quickly expanded to the rest of his body. Jack stilled, hoping to hear footsteps. The sound of foot shuffles came right for him, and Jack prepared to be bowled over. The impact didn't hit his body like he expected, but his eyes. A powder dispersed around his face, getting into his eyes, nose, and mouth.

He coughed and hacked, trying to get the particulates out of his lungs, then he rubbed his eyes. "Shit," he said when his eyes began to burn. Once they opened, he couldn't see a thing. Complete blackness surrounded him.

He felt something on his back and took a grab at it. His hand grasped Pablos's wrist.

"Pablo?"

"Stop looking for me." Pablo pulled his arm out of Jack's grasp right when a door opened behind them.

"Hey, you lost or something?" a man's voice said.

Running sounds faded in the distance. Pablo got away again.

"I can't see," Jack finally said to the man. He turned toward him.

"Damn, your eyes are red. You on some kind of new drug?"

Jack sighed. "No. I…" He needed to think fast. "I just got hot sauce in my eyes, and it finally hit me. Can I get some water to flush my eyes?"

The man grabbed Jack's arm and led him inside. "You don't smell drunk. Don't make me regret this."

Almost ten minutes later, Jack could finally see, well, mostly see. The vision around the periphery still appeared dark.

Pablo had a good start on him, but he wouldn't let him get away. Rummaging in his pockets, he searched for the locator. When it didn't turn up, he remembered he had it in his hand when he turned the corner to find Pablo vanishing.

He thanked the shop owner, gave him a twenty for his trouble, and stepped back into the alley. Half an hour later, he conceded defeat. He'd lost the locator. Someone must have picked it up.

The last person he wanted to call was the seer. He'd be pissed Jack lost it. It would be even worse if Pablo picked it up.

The potion and the powder were magic items most werewolf packs didn't carry. The pack must be in contact with a coven. If the coven gets their hand on the tracker, they will know exactly the work around the seer used to find Pablo. Shit. He needed to make his way back to the hotel and give Frank a call.

~

Emma

Emma ended her call with Jack just as she parked across from Herbs and Healing of Savannah. She canceled her date after a phone call from Ethan. She rescheduled for brunch on Saturday. The three full moons of the month started tomorrow night, so her nights were off limits until after Sunday. Pablo's one run in with the Brotherhood just became two.

She walked over to Maggie's shop. Maggie's great-grandmother Gigi converted the old two-story house into a magic shop.

The building always looked unassuming. A long porch ran the entire length of the front. The second door installed for Jesi's new law firm, now housed on the second floor, looked like it had always been there. Behind the door to Herbs and Healing laid a space filled with magic, so much so that Emma could feel it. It normally caressed her skin like feathers blowing past her.

Today, she knew it would feel like a rough blanket scratching her skin. The worry from everyone changed how the magic felt. She took a deep breath. It wouldn't keep her out, though. It never did. She'd get used to the feeling soon enough.

Bells chimed as she walked through the door. Pablo sat with his mate, Hayley, behind the counter while Ethan, Isaiah, Ms. Sylvia, and Maggie spoke in hushed voices.

None of them looked up as she approached, but Ethan pulled her close when she was within reach. There on the counter sat a flat round object, no bigger than a half dollar. In fact, if she didn't inspect it, she might have mistaken it for one.

"What exactly are we looking at?" Emma asked.

When Maggie picked it up, the entire disc turned

green. On instinct, Emma took a step back. The green flash narrowed down to a single green line that pointed from the center out. Maggie moved the coin, and the line seemed to follow a fixed point.

"Want to try it?" Maggie held it out to Emma.

She took it with a frown and walked around the shop. The line moved around the coin to keep pointing in a fixed direction, much like a magnet. She looked in the direction it pointed. With a thought, she moved into the workshop. The line pointed behind her, inside the shop. She walked out of the room and up to Pablo and Hayley.

"I'm guessing it points to Pablo." Emma raised an eyebrow at the group huddled around the counter.

"That is correct," Maggie said with a half grin. "Ethan, tell her what she's won."

The annoyed look on Ethan's face didn't stop Maggie from continuing.

"That's right, Ethan. She's won a seat at the strategy table right here in Herbs and Healing. And if things go according to plan, dinner."

Emma grinned at her friend and handed the disc back to her. "I thought you blocked Pablo's aura or whatever, so no one would track him."

"You are not wrong," Ms. Sylvia said. "How this device works is the question."

"Well, how does your block work?" Emma sat at the counter, then looked back to see Pablo resting his head on Hayley's shoulder.

"The block works like a phase shield," Maggie chimed in. "If someone's trying to find Pablo, the search will come up empty because it can't 'see' him. They can't put more power behind it either, because we've placed his trackable location on a different plane or phase."

"How very Star Trek." Emma nudged Maggie's shoulder. "What an impressive shield."

"Thank you," Ms. Sylvia said with force, her eyes narrowed on Emma.

"Damn, Ms. Sylvia's pulling out the skills." Emma went to high five Ms. Sylvia, but Ms. Sylvia shook her head.

"We were discussing this device's potential to function despite our shield." Ms. Sylvia drummed her fingers on the counter.

"We've tested it and it's not interacting with the shield at all. So, nothing has destroyed what we've created, and nothing has attacked it." Maggie flipped it like a coin, and Ms. Sylvia rolled her eyes. The green line disappeared when it left Maggie's hand and stayed gone as it landed on the countertop.

"Is it using a different type of magic?" Emma picked it up again and smelled it. So many of them had held the object. It was hard to denote a scent that didn't belong to someone in the room.

"The magic used is of witches," Ms. Sylvia said.

"I still think we should try my idea." Maggie looked at Ms. Sylvia, her eyes wide like she wanted to force her to agree.

"You speak of a last resort option." Ms. Sylvia didn't even look at Maggie.

"What's the idea?" Emma asked.

"It's an exposure spell. It'll break down the spell used into all of its parts, kind of like reverse engineering." Maggie dragged over a book Emma hadn't noticed on the far side of the top.

"What's the downside?" It sounded like the perfect solution, but there must be a problem if Ms. Sylvia considered it a last resort.

Maggie shrugged. "It will destroy the object."

A smile spread across Emma's face. "No big deal, right?"

"Exactly," Maggie agreed. "This is about keeping Pablo safe, not about preserving this object."

Ms. Sylvia's fingers drummed faster, and her face pinched tight. Emma could hear her teeth grinding. Ethan placed his hand over the coven leader's fingers. She snatched her hand away from his and placed them in her lap. Emma had seen her fuss at Maggie for drumming her own fingers over the years and didn't like to be called out on her own habit.

"Maybe they're tracking him differently," Emma suggested. "Something specific, like his inner wolf or his liver."

"I could go for some chicken livers." Maggie rubbed her stomach.

"Me too. Or Chinese," Emma said. Her stomach growled in response.

"Do they make kung pao chicken livers?" Maggie pulled out her phone and began typing.

"Ladies," Ethan said, "let's get back on track. Could Emma be onto something?"

"It is impossible for him to be tracked using any portion of his physical being," Sylvia said. Her eyes darted over to Maggie's phone. She must be hungry as well.

"So, something he wears all the time, then?" Emma picked up the disc, saw it come alive with a green flash, and then looked over at Pablo.

His head still rested on Hayley's shoulder, his hand loosely held hers, and his breathing had slowed.

"He's asleep," Hayley whispered. "But he doesn't wear jewelry. He doesn't wear any one item every day. He doesn't even have a tattoo."

Emma turned back to the group and looked at the coin again. She expected to see the green line again, but only a green dot appeared in the middle. She turned it over and over again. Nothing changed. Just a green dot.

"Did I break it?" She held it out to the group.

They all leaned in. Ms. Sylvia grabbed it, but it stayed the same. She tapped it with a finger, mumbling under her breath, to no avail. Maggie disappeared into the workshop and came back with a few herbs. Her aunt held her hand out while Maggie crushed and sprinkled the mixture over the coin.

"Power Reveal," Ms. Sylvia said. The disc flashed green, then the light turned back into a line that circled around the coin like a radar screen. After three turns, the line once again became a dot.

"Well," Maggie said with a frown. "They didn't turn it off."

"Does that mean he's safe?" Hayley asked.

Her voice woke up Pablo, whose head shot up off her

shoulder. "Sorry. I've been having trouble sleeping since Saturday."

The stress and fear obviously took its toll on the werewolf. After his experience with Cernunnos, it was a wonder he could sleep at all.

"The line is back." Maggie poked the coin still in her aunt's hand.

"Did it come back when he woke up?" Ethan asked. He stared down at the coin, then up at the coven leader. "What would that mean?"

"Consciousness," Ms. Sylvia said. It looked like a light bulb went off in her head as she stared at the device.

Maggie shot out from behind the counter and around the entire shop. She pulled books from the workshop and the room labeled 'Real Magic.' Herbs, gemstones, and salt followed. Once it was all piled on the table, she passed out the books. "There's something in one of these books that will help. I remember reading it a while back, but I don't remember which book it's in. Here's hoping it's not in the library because I still don't have access to it from here."

She flipped open a book. "Look for something to do with consciousness or the spiritual mind. Or maybe dreams and consciousness, or how our consciousness wanders while we sleep."

Ms. Sylvia stood up and dropped the coin. "I know the book. It's in the library."

"What are we going to do with the information?" Ethan asked. He continued to skim the book he held.

"If they're tracking his consciousness, we can copy

it." Maggie stood up, her eyes big and a smile threatened to form.

"We can copy its signature," Ms. Syliva clarified. "And set a trap."

"Are we using the signature as bait or me?" Pablo looked at Ethan.

"The signature, of course." The lead witch put on a light coat and her purse.

"Where will I go?" Pablo looked at his mate.

"Ethan?" Sylvia pointedly looked at him, then walked out the door, the sound of her clicking heels in her wake.

"I suppose she expects me to have an answer." Ethan smirked at the group. "I'll contact the pack over in Macon. They'll no doubt let you spend the full moons there. But it would be best if you leave sooner rather than later. Let me call her."

"I'm going too," Hayley told him as he walked off to make the call.

"Of course."

"Everyone keep looking through the books. I don't want to mess this up." Maggie tapped on the books. "The full moons start tomorrow night, and we don't want to leave Pablo and Hayley in Macon for too long. Once we figure out the magic stuff, then we can work on the fun stuff. Traps."

Maggie's smile was accompanied by what Emma liked to call her 'crazy eyes.' Emma snorted and started looking through the book in front of her.

Trap. They would set a trap. And finally, find out how the Brotherhood fit into all of this.

Chapter 12

Emma

Emma stood on a low branch of an old oak tree. From here, she could see into the forest and how the moonlight filtered through the leaves. This was the perfect night to just sit and look at the sky. Perfect jeans and t-shirt weather and just cool enough to entertain lighting a bonfire. But she stood in a tree waiting for their trap to work.

A deep breath revealed nothing and no one. She couldn't scent anything new in the area. Spencer had a better time of it. His sense of smell was the best of the pack's. He stood on the other side of the decoy. Ethan stood between the decoy and the path to the pack's enclosure. And Ethan stationed Sally, a wolf who's been in the pack almost as long as Ethan, across from himself. Spencer suggested they have more people for this task, but Ethan shot that idea down.

She looked east through the trees again. That direction was closest to the road and the most likely path the person would come from, right past Spencer. If she turned her head a little to the left, she could see her brother crouching on a branch roughly six feet from the ground. He swiveled his head back and forth. She could almost hear him sniffing the air.

Crickets and frogs sang all around them. The soothing cadence had her relaxing just enough to let her mind wander. Her thoughts drifted to Jack. Spencer had met Jack, but she hadn't told him Jack was her mate. Would they ultimately get along? Her chest tightened. While Jack stood a few inches taller than Spencer, her brother was deceptively strong. One of the side effects of lycanthropy.

A call from the north caught her attention. Sally must have caught sight of something. Before Emma could set eyes on Sally through the trees, she heard the sounds of a scuffle. She jumped from branch to branch until a leap to the ground put her on the right path.

Emma used her nose to narrow down her search. Grunts and growls echoed around her. Sally's scent mixed with a load of pepper filled the air, so she headed in that direction. A loud pop sound, followed by angry growls, sent Emma sprinting faster than before. She burst through the trees. Sally's wolf lay on the ground and a man crawled away from her. His leg bled, but Emma still could not smell him.

Emma jumped on the man within seconds and pushed him into the ground. He shook her off, but she rolled into a crouching stance. He whipped his head around, pulled out a baton one uses for self-defense, and the moonlight shone down on him. A gasp escaped Emma's lips, and her eyes grew wide.

"Jack," she whispered.

Jack's face echoed her surprise. He stumbled back and stuck the telescoping stick out toward her.

"You shot her." Emma's voice sounded foreign, even to her. The deep, gravelly sound reminded her of the night her father died, when her wolf pushed forward for the first time. She had more control now than she did back then.

"She bit me," he said through heavy breaths. "Besides, it's a tranq gun."

"It doesn't explain why you're here."

"Doesn't explain why you're here either." He took a step backward, favoring the non-bitten leg.

"I can't let you leave." Emma stood and shifted forward onto the balls of her feet. Mate or no mate, they needed answers. She needed answers.

"What makes you think you can make me stay?" He swirled the baton in his hand, took another step back, and glanced behind him.

She smelled Spencer before he let himself be known. His quiet footsteps took him to Sally's body. "She's alive," Spencer said, causing Jack to jump and aim the baton toward her kneeling brother.

"You need to come with us." Emma straightened her back. Her eyes narrowed on Jack.

"I can't let that happen."

Jack swung the baton at Emma. She caught the stick as she growled and ripped it out of his hand. A step to the right helped her dodge a punch but didn't stop her from clocking Jack in the face.

"Don't play with him," Spencer called to her. "I'm ready for a nap."

Emma grabbed Jack's arm during his next jab and twisted it behind him. She slammed his chest into a tree. Her hand tingled where she touched him. A sure sign of some sort of magic. Spencer stopped beside her.

"Normally, you'd be dead right now, but we have a few questions for you." Emma dug her nails into his wrist, and he cried out in response. With his arm twisted behind him, she pulled everything out of his pockets. Bear spray, a stun gun, and a pocketknife all fell to the ground around him while he struggled against her hold.

"Ease up." Jack's voice rang true to her ears. "You heard him. The wolf's not dead. Besides, it bit me. I'm one of you now, right?"

She leaned into his ear and said, "You should be so lucky."

"Oh. Here's a taser with the probes deployed," Spencer said. "Taser didn't work too well if he had to use a tranq gun and bear spray, as we can all smell. My eyes are starting to burn."

Ethan arrived, circled them, and casually began picking up everything Emma pulled from Jack's pockets. "You have a nice variety of defensive weapons. An interesting choice when entering a werewolf pack's territory," he said.

Jack's eyes focused on Ethan, but he said nothing. Ethan was still in his professor clothes, as he called them. Slacks, a button-down shirt with the sleeves rolled up, and boots.

"I do hope you'll cooperate. You seem like an interesting fellow. A hunter with only defensive weapons. This is one for the books."

"Does this mean we're not going to kill him?" Spencer asked. He leaned back on his heels and crossed his arms, giving Ethan a large frown.

Ethan raised his eyebrows at Spencer, then smiled at Jack. "Blind fold him and bring him along."

Emma's brother wrapped a bandana around Jack's eyes, then handed Emma the rope to tie Jack's hands. "Send someone back to help me carry her, will ya?" Spencer said, referring to carrying Sally back to the enclosure.

"Sure thing." Emma tugged Jack off the tree after securing his hands and followed behind Ethan pulling Jack along with her.

"Emma, is this really you?" Jack asked.

"Are you really chasing after werewolves?"

"Just the one."

"The one who got away? I don't believe you're Pablo's type."

"I can't believe you're a werewolf."

"And I can't believe you're a hunter."

"Well, I'm a werewolf now."

"Not for long."

"Is he really going to kill me?"

Emma laughed. "He doesn't normally do the killing."

They walked through the forest in silence, with Emma keeping Jack from falling from every branch and hole in the way. Emma's heart cracked with each step toward the enclosure. By the time she led him into their single holding room, which usually held extra blankets and pillows, she could barely keep her tears from falling.

She closed the door behind him and leaned against it. Her fated mate stood inches from her, yet miles away.

She heard his soft voice through the closed door. "Who normally does the killing?"

"I do." Then she walked away.

~

Jack

Emma didn't untie his hands when she left, though she took the blindfold off. Jack looked around the small cell, or rather, room. The empty space contained a single light that was on. The floor and one wall looked like concrete and the other walls were drywall. The white paint could use a fresh coat, but at least it didn't look dirty.

The adrenaline he felt faded away. His leg throbbed, and he looked down to see it still bleeding all over his shoe. The concrete floor soaked up the blood that fell. With little options, he backed up to a wall and carefully slid down it, his injured leg resting straight out in front of him. Maybe he would leave them with a bloody leg print on the floor. All he could do now was wait.

Chapter 13

Emma

Emma hovered near the room that held Jack. She paced the concrete floor of the tunnel between the home she grew up in and the enclosure where the pack shifted during the full moon.

Her father built the underground tunnel as a 'just in case escape plan' as well as a way to stay dry when it rained. The long hallway held a handful of rooms usually used for storing items not used regularly. Cubbies like you'd find in a fancy mud room lined the halls for personal items, and chests filled with pillows and blankets sat beside those. Keon pulled the rolling rack of towels down the hall, which they normally kept in the room before she put Jack in it.

The wolf in her head nudged her and begged to go to Jack. Stupid wolf. She stayed quiet for years and now wants to take over. The wolf would have to wait. Not even having a mate would force Emma to shift. She was also too confused and mad to go in there alone.

Spencer walked up to her, holding a first aid kit in one hand and handcuffs in the other. "Let's go keep our prisoner from getting an infection. We should have just killed him."

Emma grabbed her brother's arm. "We can't."

He must have heard the desperation in her voice because he looked at her like he didn't know her.

"What do you mean, 'we can't?' I know you went on a few dates with him, but really? You ignore orders all the time."

"He's…" She didn't want to say it. Saying it made it real. She closed her eyes and let go of his arm. "He's my mate."

Her body suddenly felt heavy. Her shoulders sagged, and she couldn't look Spencer in the eye. Fate matched her with a monster.

"Fuck." Spencer pulled her into a hug, and she sunk into her brother's embrace. "That guy? What's his name again?"

"Jack."

"I won't kill him then. Does Ethan know?"

She stepped back. "No. Not yet."

"Let's patch him up, then talk to Ethan. Maybe you can convince him to talk while we're in there."

She walked into the room first. Jack sat on the floor with his long legs stretched out in front of him. Blood pooled around his calf.

His head leaned back on the wall behind him, eyes

closed. He didn't open them when they arrived, like he couldn't sense the danger of his situation.

"First things first," Spencer said. "Let's secure the hunter."

This caused Jack to crack an eye open. They both kneeled beside him and untied his hands. Spencer put one handcuff on Jack but landed on his ass when Jack punched him in the face and scrambled to the door.

Emma pulled him back to the wall and secured his other hand in the handcuff.

"Damnit, he punched me." Spencer rubbed his eye. "Do you think it's going to bruise? I don't want Clare to worry."

"You just don't want her to know you got nailed by a human. Just wait till I tell Keon."

"Low blow. He'll never let me live it down."

Emma watched as Jack tried to scoot his way past them again. He reached the door, pulled it open, and bounced back into the room. He tried again but couldn't make it through the door due to the invisible barrier that interacted with the handcuffs. It was one of Maggie's clever ideas.

Jack turned to look at them. "How do you have this kind of magic?"

"Why are you attempting to escape while bleeding to death?" Emma clasped his arm and led him back to where they found him sitting. "Have a seat and we'll stop the bleeding."

He fell more than sat back down. "Do you even know what you're doing? Why would you even bother?"

Emma raised her eyebrow with a frown on her lips. "I am a vet, remember? And Spencer here is a phlebotomist."

He looked between Spencer and her as Spencer pulled what they needed out of the first aid kit. "You did mention your brother was a phlebotomist."

"Awe, you talk about me?" Spencer grinned like a madman at her. "You love me, don't you?"

"I hate you at the moment." She took the scissors and cut away the bottom half of his pants leg to the knee. "So, you want to enlighten us as to why you're looking for Pablo?"

"You going to tell me how you set up that trap?"

"We're obviously good at magic," Spencer said right as he poured an antiseptic cleanser over his leg.

Jack stayed quiet while they worked. Emma felt a sort of pride that he didn't complain when she gave him a few stitches. Her fellow pack mates always whined and complained if she had to stitch them up. Of course, her pack mates didn't have to prove anything to her and maybe Jack felt differently. Happy panting filled her head when her wolf once again came to the forefront of her mind. Her wolf's feelings differed from her human feelings. She had never felt so out of sync before.

After they cleaned up, Spencer left the room. Emma leaned against the opposite wall of where Jack sat.

"So, you must have been born a werewolf." He stared at the floor.

"Is that a question?"

"An observation. Were you ever going to tell me?"

She crossed her arms. "You need to answer my questions, not the other way around."

His eyes flickered to hers. "You're going to kill me, anyway. Why should I talk?"

"What a wild assumption. I don't patch up people just to watch them die."

He stared back at her then. She could almost hear the gears in his head turning.

"Then... what are you going to do to me?"

"That depends on your answers."

~

Jack

He watched Emma leave the room only for the older man with the slacks to walk in with two chairs. He set them both up, then offered his hand to pull Jack up. After a moment of staring at his outstretched hand, Jack grabbed it. The man helped Jack into a plastic seat, then sat on the other across from him.

"My name is Ethan, and I am the leader of this pack." Ethan reached into his pocket and pulled out a vial. "Please drink this."

Jack took the vial out of his hands. "What is this?"

"That is the antidote for the bite on your leg. You only have up to forty-eight hours after a bite until it no longer works."

Jack looked at the potion in his hand. The blue liquid sloshed around as he inspected it. "I don't know what this is, but there is no antidote. The supposed key ingredient doesn't exist; therefore, the antidote is a fabrication."

He let it drop from his hand and it crashed on the floor, sending blue liquid splashing on the concrete with his blood stains. The sound of Ethan's loud sigh caught Jack's attention. Ethan pressed his thumb and forefinger on the bridge of his nose between his eyes.

"Emma," he called out.

Emma's head poked through the door.

"Do we have any more of the antidote?"

"No." She looked down at the mess, then glared at Jack. "I'll call Maggie in the morning. If she's out, the earliest we can get some is late-morning or early afternoon."

She left before Jack could say anything. He stared at the mess he'd created and frowned. What could they possibly be trying to give him? He wasn't all that important in the grand scheme of things and with the bite on his leg, they must know his best option is to cooperate.

The sound of Ethan clearing his throat brought Jack's attention back. The older man frowned. "I suppose we can move on. I understand your name is Jack."

"Yes."

"Why exactly were you trespassing?"

Jack's instinct was to wince at the terminology, but he knew better than to show weakness. What he said was true, so he couldn't argue. He took a deep breath and hoped they could come to an understanding if he told the truth.

"I'm looking for someone. An old roommate. I only want to talk to him."

"Oh. Did he skip town without paying rent?"

"No."

"Did he steal from you?"

Jack shook his head.

"What could you possibly want to talk to him about?" Ethan looked confused and curious. He either had a wonderful poker face or honestly didn't have a clue. Jack bet on the former. They didn't set up a trap for no reason.

The door cracked open again, and Emma stood there with a broom. "Mind if I get this off the floor?"

Ethan nodded. She walked in and quickly cleaned up the scattered shards of glass. She turned to leave sooner than Jack wanted. The small smile she gave him when she opened the door to leave wrapped around his heart.

"Can she stay?" he asked. The thought didn't even process in his brain before it came out of his mouth. As surprised as he was to hear himself ask, he knew he wouldn't take it back. He wanted her there to hear what he had to say in person.

Ethan raised an eyebrow at him, then turned to Emma. "Why would he ask that?"

Emma leaned over and whispered something in his ear, too quiet for Jack to hear. The old man's eyes widened, then he shook his head. "Well, go get a chair."

She slipped out of the room and returned thirty seconds later, setting up a chair beside Ethan.

"Jack here was about to tell us why he wanted to talk to his former roommate," Ethan said.

"And who is the former roommate?" Emma asked, her face suddenly blank.

A smile crept up on Jack's face. Her innocent act looked adorable but it was the last thought he should have as a prisoner. "Pablo. Pablo was my roommate over a year ago. He left suddenly, and he stopped responding to my texts."

"You've been looking for him for over a year?" Ethan asked.

"No." Jack dropped his head. "My best friend is also a werewolf. We grew up together. A few months after Pablo left, my friend disappeared. He didn't tell his parents or the pack leader. I started calling around to other packs close by, then expanded to those further out. I noticed a trend. One or two members of a good number of the packs were missing. Just picked up and left. Some left empty homes, others left everything behind. One or two missing people is bad enough, but when that number keeps growing, then…"

"How many?" Emma asked.

"At my last count, thirty-two. Thirty-two missing werewolves."

"What process did you follow in the search?"

Jack took a deep breath and let it out. "We tracked their social media, their bank accounts, cars…You name it, we traced it. It took months. We got a potential lead a few months ago, but nothing significant. I hired five different psychics and seers. They cycle through the names and pictures we gave them every few weeks. Finally, one tried a unique method and located Pablo."

"They tracked his consciousness," Ethan said.

Jack couldn't stop his surprise. "How did you…"

"Pablo picked up your tracking device." Emma leaned forward. "Who is 'we?'"

"We?" Jack asked.

"You said, 'we traced it' and 'we got a potential lead.' Who's we?" She stared straight into his eyes.

"The Brotherhood. But I bet you already knew that. Pablo knew that. I told him about us."

"That he did," Ethan said. "But the details he has are a bit fuzzy. So, what exactly do you want from Pablo and who exactly is the Brotherhood?"

Jack looked at Emma. The blank face she had on a moment ago was gone, replaced with a frown and worry lines on her forehead. He wanted to kiss them away and tell her everything would work out, even if she punched him in the face again. So, he took a deep breath and began at the beginning.

Chapter 14

Emma

Jack talked. His eyes glazed a bit like he'd either spoken these words or heard them a thousand times. "Thousands of years ago, humans and the supernatural world clashed. They equally feared and despised each other. The bloodshed and power struggle between the two eventually led to an all-out war. A group of humans and the supernatural came together to stand between the two worlds and provide a compromise. They alone kept the two from fighting by stopping those individuals' hell bent on destroying the other. That group grew over the years. It expanded over the continents. Some remained connected while others branched off on their own, all with the common goal of finding and keeping a balance between the humans and the supernaturals.

"The Brotherhood is one of those groups. No one knows if it was the original group or not, but at this point, it doesn't matter. The Brotherhood had great success in maintaining the balance of the world. They hunted down humans who wished to expose or kill supernaturals and hunted down supernaturals who wanted to control or kill humans. This system worked well. The many hunter groups expanded, worked together, and helped each of the groups.

"About two hundred years ago, a man named Trevor Belmont took over one of the larger organizations, Guardians of Pínghéng, and corrupted it from the inside. His anger stemmed from the death of his parents at the hands of rogue werebears in the mountains of what's now Hungary. He claimed that if werebears were willing to do something as grizzly as attack witches, what else would they do? Who else would they attack? So, the Guardians of Pínghéng started to track down and kill werebears. But it didn't stop there. Next were the werewolves and the human hybrids, then witches. Belmont came from a long line of witches, which confused those under him as they twisted the organization's purpose. Belmont renounced his witch background and set forth to rid his group of all supernaturals, saying that no one should have such a clear advantage over the other.

"More of the hunter groups joined the cause, and the supernaturals went into hiding, masking their scent and using new magics to hide. Only a few hunter groups stuck to the old ways. They were cast aside as non-progressive, but they stood for balance, not bloodshed.

"The Brotherhood is one of them. We managed to

keep one branch open on each continent. We do what we can to keep the supernatural safe from the humans and the humans safe from the supernatural. The last hundred years have been difficult to maintain and build positive relationships with supernatural packs, covens, and groups."

"What happened to the Guardians of Pínghéng?" Emma asked.

"They're still around. We've heard rumbles of one of their branches falling into new hands with a name change. There is speculation as to the new name, but nothing concrete."

"I'd heard most of the story of the hunters turning on their sworn duty. I guess we'll have to wait to see if what you told us is true." Ethan stood up and brushed off the front of his pants like they could be dirty.

"Truth potion." Jack shook his head.

"Nope," Emma said with a smirk. "We have something even better."

Emma watched Jack's brow furrow when he mentioned a truth potion, and how it relaxed once she refuted his assumption. She suddenly wanted to see how he reacted to a truth potion. Of course, Jesi was the better option, and she got back from her cruise yesterday.

"Thank you for your time," Ethan said. "I do hope you're telling the truth. We will be back in the morning."

Ethan folded up his chair and nodded at Emma to do the same. She followed his unspoken request and followed him out of the room. Before the door closed behind her, she turned to see Jack staring at her with puppy dog eyes. That look could be a trick for all she knew.

Once the door shut, Ethan took her chair and said, "Go grab him some blankets. It's not exactly cold, but we're not monsters. I'll call Sylvia before I contact Jesi if you talk to Maggie. We'll talk more in the morning."

She watched him walk away. His hair began to grow. She knew he'd put away the chairs and shift to spend time with the pack. As much as she'd like to spend time with the pack as well, she couldn't deny the pull toward Jack. Stupid moon. She couldn't even shift, and she still felt the effects of the mate bond.

Rummaging through the various trunks that lined the hallways, she found a good stack of blankets, even a few soft ones to protect him from the floor and a pillow. Before she opened the door, she sent a quick text to Maggie to call when she woke up. As much as she wanted to drag her best friend out of bed now, she knew Maggie needed her rest for potion making tomorrow.

When she walked in, Jack hadn't moved from the chair. His eyes looked tired, and his face pale. She placed her pile on the floor near the door. "I'll help you put together a pallet on the floor."

She pulled out the softest blanket and spread it out on the section of floor without blood and potion. He limped over and helped spread it out. After a few minutes, the blankets were all down in a makeshift bed.

"I don't suppose you have a different pair of pants for me to wear." He gave her a weak smile.

She reached out and touched his cheek before she could stop herself. His stubble bit into her hand when he leaned into it. She wanted to believe him. If the Brotherhood was indeed holding up the old ways, then they could work together, and she could trust Jack.

The more she looked at him, head in her hand, she realized she trusted him, anyway. She pulled him into a hug, her arms wrapped around his upper body, holding his head to her neck. His cuffed hands dug into her belly. With a sigh, she pulled back.

He slowly lifted his arm, and she slipped between his bound arms. She pulled him close, stuck her nose into his neck and breathed him in. This close, his natural scent of cedar, jasmine, and vanilla soothed her. Whatever he used to hide his scent started to wear off. His arms surrounded her, their bodies pressed together enough for her to feel his broken breathing. She felt his wet tears land on her shoulder. They stood there, holding each other tighter than before. Afraid she'd bruise his ribs with her fingers, she loosened her hold.

"Not yet," he whispered. "Just hold me a little longer." His fingers pulled at her shirt as he dug his face deeper into her neck.

She slowly rubbed his back. "It's okay. I'll stay as long as I can."

Time became meaningless as they held each other. Emma wondered if he felt as relieved as she did now that they'd shared their big secrets. Not that she wanted him to find out that way, and she had more to tell, but he'd gone through enough today.

She wanted to take his handcuffs off and lay down with him on the blankets. The enclosure had nothing she needed or wanted more than the man in this room. And yet, would she choose him over the pack if it came to that choice?

His breathing slowed as she supported more and more of his weight.

"Jack," she whispered. "Jack. You're falling asleep."

"Hum?" He startled in that half-awake way, and his knees buckled.

Emma kept him from hitting the ground. "Here. Let's get you on the blankets."

She untangled herself from his arms and lowered him down by grabbing his hands. He sat on the blankets with crisscrossed legs and heavy eyes. "I'm sorry."

"What are you sorry for?" Emma crouched down.

"For everything. I've been so desperate for information about Dakota that I'm making rash decisions. I told myself I'd only look to see if Pablo was here and maybe come back in the morning, but I'm sure I'd probably try to talk to him if I saw him. Which is dumb. He wasn't born a werewolf. He can't shift into a human during a full moon."

Emma patted his cheek. "He's not here. And he can shift back and forth during a full moon."

"What? I thought…"

"He shouldn't be able to. If your friend is going through anything close to what happened to Pablo, you have every right to be concerned. For now, rest, and I'll see you in the morning."

"Now my imagination is running wild." He fiddled with his cuffs with a frown. "Thank you for staying and for the blankets. I hate that this is the way you found out about my actual job or other job. I do help my sister out with the hotel business when she needs it."

"I hate that this is how you found out about me. And I might be sorry about the shiner you'll have in the morning. Might not. I'll need to see how Sally's doing."

"Fair enough." He reached over and gently lifted her hand to his mouth, kissing her knuckles. "I'd walk you to the door, but I don't know if I can get up at the moment."

"Good night, Jack," Emma whispered. She leaned over and gave him a quick kiss, then made her way to the door before he could react. "I'll be back in the morning."

He nodded, and she left. She made her way to the enclosure with Jack on her mind. Even if everything he told them today was true, she still knew she shouldn't trust him. The entire pack, especially Ethan and Spencer, would remind her what he was. A hunter. The kind of person she'd protected this pack against repeatedly over the last decade.

She looked out through the forest and watched her pack mates romp around while others slept in a pile of warmth. Her heart wanted Jack here. Jack was both a threat and her mate all at once. The one person she should walk away from was the one person she needed to walk toward.

A howl sounded through the night, and she looked

up at the sky full of stars. How would she get her heart to agree with logic, or convince her brain to throw logic to the wind?

Chapter 15

Emma

Emma didn't get much sleep on the cushions in the building that led to the underground tunnel. Normally, she pulled on a pair of thick sweatpants and a sweatshirt and curled up with one of the wolf piles to sleep. Last night she couldn't go out. Her heart made her a traitor. It pulled her to leave and go to Jack. And her mind forced her to stay put.

Climbing out of the heap of her makeshift bed of cushions and blankets, she cleaned up and rushed off to grab breakfast. Wes danced around the kitchen, making breakfast with Keon. She snatched a plate and filled it up, then moved to leave.

"Where are you going?" Wes asked.

She looked over at Keon, but he just swayed on his feet like he might fall back asleep while cooking bacon.

"Uh, we caught the guy looking for Pablo." She lifted

the plate. "I was going to feed him."

"I heard." Wes gave her a knowing look. "I also smelled him this morning."

She frowned and shifted from foot to foot. He knew what Jack was to her, but she wasn't ready for everyone to jump into her business.

"Don't worry," Wes said. "My lips are sealed. If you need to talk, let me know."

"Thanks Wes."

She walked out into the hallway when she heard Keon say, "Talk about what?"

Once she made it to the door, she could smell Jack now as well. Whatever spell or potion he'd used last night to cover his scent had worn off completely. The pull toward him grew the more she could smell him. That cedar, vanilla, and jasmine combo put fantasies of her burying her face in his neck and chest, and... other places. No matter what, she wouldn't drop to her knees when she walked in. Not now anyway.

Jack sat on the pallet of blankets leaning against the wall when she walked into the room. He smiled at her and visibly relaxed.

"Were you worried?" She asked.

"No." He looked down. "Actually yes. I kept hearing people walking by the door, expecting them to burst in, seeking retribution."

He accepted the plate she held out. "Only a few people are allowed to interact with... uh, you."

He raised an eyebrow. "Prisoners? Is that the word you're looking for?"

"Yes," she said with a grimace. What a terrible word to call him, but he spoke the truth. Right now, he was a prisoner.

She kneeled beside him and touched his face. "I have to go. I'll be back, though, and with the antidote. Ethan will be here once our lie detector arrives."

"What is this lie detector anyway if it's not a truth potion?"

"Something similar, but different. Don't worry, it can't hurt you."

He grabbed her hand on his cheek and kissed her palm. "Okay. I trust you."

"Do you think that's a good idea?"

His eyes widened in shock, then narrowed. "Yes. I do think it's a good idea."

Her heart clenched in delight or regret. She didn't know. With a light kiss to his lips, she walked out of the room to look for Spencer, then headed to Maggie's.

~

Jack

That morning, Jack had little time to spend with Emma. She dropped off breakfast and promised that the lie detector was on the way. It made little sense to him because lie detectors often gave false readings. She cupped his cheek and told him she'd be back with the antidote. He didn't dispute her claim of an antidote and kissed her palm before she left.

When he tried to sleep the night before, he thought

about her. He had never felt so strongly about anyone, and never so quickly. At first, he told himself that she was just a fun distraction while he searched for Pablo, but the way he looked for her as he traveled around Savannah told a different story. It didn't take long for him to realize he wanted to see her more. Even his sister picked up on it. He missed Emma, even when he knew she was close by.

An hour later, Spencer came in with an arm full of folding chairs. He set each one up, then sat in one with a sigh. Jack pulled himself up from his seat on the floor and sat in the same chair he occupied earlier.

"What's all this?" Jack motioned to the chairs.

"The lie detector is here." Spencer leaned back. "Let me ask you something. You think you'll keep dating my sister after this?"

"Are you going to give me the 'hurt her and I'll kill you talk' if I do?"

"You're going to get that talk either way. But it won't just be me who comes after you." He smiled at Jack, showing off his canines. "This entire pack loves Emma. We rely on her more than she realizes. She could be the next pack leader, but she questions her abilities. So, if you hurt her, no one will ever find your remains. Not even your witch that tracked down Pablo."

Jack kept eye contact with Spencer the entire time he spoke, even when Spencer's eyes turned golden, showing the wolf inside. The love that surrounded Emma made Jack happy. Happy because her support system saw her for her true worth. And he would give anything to see her for who she truly was.

"Yeah," Jack said. "I'd like to keep dating her. If she'll have me."

Spencer's toothy grin relaxed into a genuine smile as he clasped Jack's shoulder. "Good man. Now let's see how you do with the next test."

Spencer turned his head, and Jack looked up to see Ethan walk through the door with a woman and a man. The lady, while not as tall as Emma, had long black hair twisted into small sections and wore jeans and a loose blouse. The man had blonde hair and a short beard and wore jeans and a plain blue t-shirt. He was only a few inches taller than the lady.

The man looked slightly familiar, and his eyes lit up as if he recognized Jack. In fact, the lady's eyes lit up in recognition as well, even though he knew he had never seen her before.

She walked over and sat down in front of him, and the man sat beside her. "Jack Bellamy. I'm Jesi and this is Chuck."

"Bellamy. As in Bellamy Hotels?" Ethan asked.

"How do you know my last name when the pack leader doesn't?" Jack narrowed his eyes and wished he could get out of the handcuffs.

Jesi bit her lip. "I have the power to glean, and I've seen you in Pablo's memories."

Jack sucked in a breath. He'd heard of gleaning, but he didn't expect this pack to have a contact with that ability. In fact, it's such a rare power for a person to know someone's entire past with a single touch, he never really considered anyone having it. One of the Brotherhood's books mentioned that only one witch at a time can possess the ability.

"Normally, I ask permission before I use my gift, but in this case, I'm afraid that's not an option."

"Why are you being so considerate?" Spencer asked. "You weren't with the last hunter."

"When was the last time?" Chuck asked.

"Remember that time I rushed out here after Haley called, and I told you that you weren't allowed to come along?" Jesi asked.

"Yes."

"Then."

"What happened then?" Chuck frowned, and his eyes widened.

That's when it hit Jack. Chuck was the man who came to see Pablo over a year ago. Chuck showing up was the reason Pablo decided to leave Winston-Salem.

"I'll tell you later." Jesi patted his knee and kissed his cheek. "And I'm being considerate because Emma asked me to."

Knowing Emma wanted this powerful witch to be nice to him made his heart flutter. Fuck, he was done for. He couldn't walk away from Emma, not for long.

"You have my permission either way," Jack said.

Jesi smiled at him. "I'm going to take your hand and hold it for anywhere from thirty seconds to five minutes."

He nodded, holding his hand out to her. She took it and closed her eyes. Her hold tightened as they watched her eyes move around behind her eyelids. Pain shot through his hand as she squeezed harder. Jack tried not to grimace while Chuck reached over and rubbed her back. Suddenly, she let go with a huge gasp. She smiled at Jack and then over at Chuck.

"Good news then?" Chuck asked.

"Yes." She looked at Ethan. "Everything you told me checks out. He's from the Brotherhood, and he has no desire to hurt Pablo. He's searching for his friend Dakota and apparently the Brotherhood is also investigating Cernunnos, but he doesn't know the progress of his co-workers."

Jack's jaw dropped. He knew she would see everything, but nothing prepared him for the reality. This woman now knew everything that had passed through his head. All his experiences. God, she knew about his obsession with Claudia Black and Serena Williams as a teen.

"He's also serious about our Emma." Jesi grinned at him with knowing eyes.

Oh god. She knew about that too. Emma's brother sitting beside him made the entire situation worse.

"Gross," Spencer said.

"And his reason for making his way here?" Ethan asked.

"Exactly what he told you. He's desperate to find his friend."

Jack gave Jesi a smile. Her power saved him.

"Well, in that case, we can take these off." Ethan stood and pulled a key out of his pocket. "Of course, we will have stipulations."

"And they are?" Jack wanted to agree to anything he said at the moment to get the cuffs off.

"First, you will agree to have your memory wiped of the location of this place." Ethan stood with his hands behind his back as if he were about to give a lecture. "Second, if you ever come back to the Savannah area, you are to call me and let me know. If you are unsure if the area you are visiting constitutes the Savannah area, call me anyway. Third, if we hear of you harming the supernatural community, you will no longer be welcome in our area, i.e., Savannah, nor in any areas with our allies."

"You realize that part of what I do is keep not only the supernatural safe from humans, but humans safe from supernaturals. I won't ignore it if humans are being attacked needlessly by the supernatural community."

"I understand and will be reasonable in my judgment of your actions," the leader said.

"Also, I don't know who your allies are."

"We will cross that bridge when we come to it." Ethan smiled at him and unlocked the cuffs.

Everyone filed out of the room while Ethan worked.

"One more thing, Jack." Ethan put his hand on Jack's shoulder. "Your actions will reflect on Emma. She vouched for you extensively last night. You are special to her. Don't break her trust."

"I wouldn't dare." He wanted nothing more than to see her at that moment. Her confidence in him settled something inside of him, like she was the direction he needed to head.

"I'd like you to stay here for a few days," Ethan continued. "We'll ask Pablo to speak with you, but I won't force him. I don't know if what he has to tell you will help or not, but I believe Cernunnos is behind both of our problems."

"Mr. Ethan, I'd like you to think about meeting with the Brotherhood to form a kind of alliance or friendship. I truly think we can help each other. Or at least I hope we can help each other."

Jack followed Ethan out of the small room and down the concrete hall.

"It sounds like an interesting idea. I'll need to talk to some of the others. I may be in charge, but I'm not a dictator. A decision like this will affect the entire pack." Ethan led him to a flight of stairs and waved him ahead.

The stairs ended in a room with two doors and a wraparound ramp leading down, presumably to the same place they'd left. Ethan walked through a door that led to a hallway in a cozy-looking home then directed him toward a dining room with a long dining table.

A person with bright blue hair stood there wiping the table down, looked up and grinned wildly at Jack. "Are you the human that clocked Spencer?"

"Uh… yeah," Jack replied.

Ethan shook his head and sat down. "This is Tick. They are on clean-up duty after breakfast." Ethan's emphasis on the word 'they' clued Jack in on how to address the person in front of him.

"I can't wait to tell Keon. How did you get a shot in?" Tick bounced a bit.

"Just a lucky shot?"

Jack looked over at Ethan. With the goodwill the leader of the pack presented to him moments before, he didn't want to risk destroying it now because of gossip.

The older man nodded at Jack's discretion as Tick frowned and continued to wipe down the table.

A door opened and closed further into the house. Tick's face lit up. "Keon," they yelled. "Come meet the human who gave Spencer a black eye."

A tall man with a short mohawk of tight, black curly hair came sliding into the room. When he laid his eyes on Jack, he smiled. "Yeah. My man." He shook Jack's hand with a laugh.

"You've given us so much ammo." Tick's eyes practically twinkled.

"What did he end up telling Clare?" Ethan asked.

Keon and Tick looked at each other, eyes wide.

"He told me he fell out of a tree." Clare, whom he met on the river a few days ago, walked out of the kitchen. Her smirk caused Keon and Tick to crack up. "It would be a good story if he had more than one bruise. Hello, Jack."

Jack shook her hand as well.

"Nice to see you again. I hear you want to continue to date my mate's sister?" She sat at the table opposite him and Ethan.

"That's why your car smells like Emma." Keon said, nudging Tick. "Here's what I grabbed from his car."

Keon placed Jack's jacket, his phone, and a small bag of toiletries he always kept in his vehicle. Ethan looked through the pile and handed Jack his jacket and bag of toiletries.

"I'll keep your phone for a bit. Can't be too careful." Ethan placed the phone in his pocket, and Jack knew he'd do the same thing if their situations were reversed.

"Do you think she'll still date you now that she knows you're a hunter?" Tick raised an eyebrow.

"I believe you two have somewhere to be," Ethan said.

Tick and Keon looked at each other, then backed away. "Yes." Tick looked at their watch. "We have practice in three hours. We don't want to be late."

They left, leaving Clare and Ethan at the table with Jack.

"What kind of practice?" Jack asked.

"We're in a band." Clare looked out the window.

"Right. With Spencer. Emma told me he was in a band. Sorry I missed your performance on Thursday."

Clare gave him a small smile, looked toward Ethan, then stood up. "Well, I need to fix something to bring to practice. Let me know if you need anything."

Ethan turned to Jack after Clare left. "I'm going to make a few phone calls. Please stay in the house for now. I won't be long, then we can have a detailed discussion about Cernunnos."

Chapter 16

Emma

Most of the cars were gone by the time Emma made it back to Spencer's house after breathing down Maggie's neck while she made more of the antidote. She walked into the house without knocking with her small bag of five antidotes Maggie gave her.

Before she left for Maggie's, Spencer took half a pint of blood from her, since Maggie couldn't make the antidote fast enough for the surrounding packs. They knew Cernunnos was behind the onslaught of attacks, but to what end, they could only guess.

Maggie teased her the entire time she made the antidote.

"So, your mate is a hunter that might be an old school hunter," Maggie said, stirring the potion. "Are you ready for him to hunt you?"

"Oh god." Emma put her head in her hands.

"Straight into the bedroom." Maggie laughed and made the worst growling noise Emma had ever heard.

"This is more fun when we team up to tease others." Emma tried to hide her smile. A little teasing wouldn't stop them from being best friends. "You just wait until you find someone."

"I'll welcome your jabs because I'll know what I have." Maggie frowned and looked at Emma. "Oh, I'm sorry, Em. I know this is hard for you because of who he is and who you are. I just want you to be happy. If you leave the pack for him, I'll back you one hundred percent."

"Will you understand, though?"

"No, but that doesn't matter. Besides, I've met him once and didn't get a bad feeling, so he's probably good. I mean, he is good looking."

"I thought you said I could do better." Emma crossed her arms.

"Well, no one is good enough for my best friend. You'll always be able to do better." Maggie leaned over and gave her a quick one-armed hug. "You could definitely do better in the brother department."

"Stop," Emma laughed. "Spencer might take that seriously from you."

"Nah."

The potion bubbled, and the color slowly changed into blue. It only had a few more minutes before it finished.

"I shouldn't trust him, you know." Her words came out softly in the small workshop at Maggie's shop. "He's a hunter. I'm a werewolf, sort of. But my heart is ready to jump in with both feet. I don't know the consequences of doing something like that. What if I jump, and I find out his morals are completely different from mine? What if his idea of interfering between humans and the supernatural means he always sides with the humans? How will my relationship with Jack affect you and Spencer and the pack? I don't want to be the one responsible for raining down destruction on my family."

Maggie pulled the cauldron off the fire to cool and gathered up the vials for storage. Emma watched Maggie's face as she thought about what Emma had said. As much as Maggie loved to tease her friends, she also knew when they needed her serious side. It's something Emma admired about her friend. It's why she thought Maggie should be the head of the coven, but no one asked for her opinion.

Once she had set up all the materials, Maggie turned to Emma. "Fate brought you two together. From the moment you two were born, a connection formed. The bond you two have works both ways, even if Jack doesn't realize it. It sounds like you're afraid he'll change you beyond recognition. That won't happen. You're Emma Luvel, protector of the Old Moss Pack. Either he accepts all of you or none of you. And if you want him, you'll have to do the same. Will you change a little? Of course. What relationship doesn't change us?

"And don't worry about the rest of us. We love you, but you've spent your entire adult life looking after us, protecting us. It's time for you to follow your heart. Your head will catch up. And if he hurts you, I'll kill him."

Now Emma walked through the front door and heard Jack before she saw him. She followed his voice and her nose and found him sitting in the dining room with Ethan.

"Hey." She sat down across from them. "You don't have handcuffs."

"Yes. Jesi corroborated his story." Ethan patted Jack's shoulder. "We were just discussing our knowledge of Cernunnos. I believe our groups could help each other out in the future."

Emma wanted to sigh in relief. She was glad her instinct about him wasn't false.

Ethan stood up. "Jack has given me the number of the leader of the Brotherhood. I'm going to call and set up a meeting. Jack has agreed to stay until Monday. Can you show him around?"

Emma nodded. Once Ethan stepped out of sight, she pulled one antidote out of the bag and handed it to Jack. "Please drink this."

He raised his eyebrow but took the vial from her hand. "Is this really an antidote for the werewolf's bite?"

"Yes, it is. And you need to take it within forty-eight hours of the bite, or it won't work."

He rolled it between his fingers. "You know, I've come across the potion recipe for this before, and one of the ingredients didn't exist."

Emma smirked. "I guess you had a bad recipe."

"Are you sure this works?"

"Of course. You're probably already exhibiting some werewolf abilities like sharper eyesight or stronger smells. I can already smell the change starting on you." His scent had hints of a werewolf undertone that she had not smelled before.

"I don't know about that." He lifted his nose and sniffed the air. "I do smell coffee with a hint of strawberries. Now I want strawberries."

Emma wondered if that scent belonged to her. "So, what was the ingredient that didn't exist?"

"What?"

"In the antidote you found. The impossible ingredient?"

"Hum... It was the blood of a carrier."

Emma smiled at him. "You know, just because you've never met a carrier, doesn't mean they don't exist."

"Wait. You know a carrier?" He sat forward in his chair, gripping the vial in his hand.

"Of course. It's not something we share with most people, nor will I tell you who it is. It can be dangerous for them if others find out."

"That makes sense. I do have questions. Like how do you find out if someone is a carrier? I don't imagine every non-werewolf child born to a werewolf is bitten just on the off chance they might be a carrier."

"That's like taking cute aggression to the extreme. Nibble all the babies." Emma laughed. She really shouldn't. "Though I'm sure it's been done in the past."

"It's a way to up the pack numbers, I suppose."

"I don't know anyone that would do that. But to answer your question, they found out when the carrier bit a classmate in elementary school and that classmate turned. From there, their pack leader ran a series of tests to confirm it, including creating the antidote."

Jack looked at the object in his hand.

"Did you know," Emma continued, "that if you try to make the antidote with the blood of anyone other than a carrier, the potion turns orange? If it's blue, then you used the correct ingredients."

Emma remembered sitting in Gigi's shop huddled with Maggie, trying to hold back her tears after finding out she changed her classmate's life forever. Even though the older witch wasn't her grandmother, she insisted Emma call her Gigi as well and, to be honest, she always treated Emma the same as she treated Maggie.

That day, Gigi made two sets of potions. One with the blood of Emma's father and another with Emma's blood. The first turned orange, and the second turned blue. It wasn't long before they had a chance to test the blue potion. Emma's self-esteem skyrocketed after the success of the antidote, though it wouldn't stamp down all her insecurities about belonging to the pack.

Jack pulled the cork on the vial. "If something weird happens, remember, I know where you live." He then downed the liquid.

"Wait!" Emma cried. "You're supposed to turn around three times and drink it while facing the west."

He jumped out of his seat and turned to her with just a hint of terror in his widened eyes, which caused her to dissolve into giggles. She leaned back in her chair, all smiles and laughs while he frowned at her with just enough of a pouting lip that she noticed.

"I'm sorry. It was just too easy."

"What if I really had to do that?" He placed the empty vial on the table with a thunk.

"You would have known the first time Ethan gave it to you."

"I can't believe you're so mean to me." He sat down, unable to hide the smile creeping up on his lips.

"What would you do if I wasn't joking?"

He shrugged. "I guess I'd be a werewolf. My best friend is one, and we grew up together. I don't think it would be that bad."

"You'd be surprised. I've seen the emotional and psychological toll the change has taken on those bitten."

"Well, I hope I'd have you to help with that."

"Are you flirting with me?"

"Always."

His smile caused her heart to speed up, and she hoped he couldn't hear it from there. The rate at which the body changed once bitten differed from person to person. Luckily, his process would stop and revert within an hour.

"I'll be honest. I'm glad you don't have to go through that. It's hard to watch someone go through that when you can't help."

"I guess you don't have to worry now."

"Yeah." She reached across and squeezed his hand. "Let me show you around."

"This is the formal dining room. The pack crams in here, the kitchen, and the living room before and after the moons to eat."

"I heard that eating a big meal before shifting helped keep tempers down."

"You would be right."

The dining room was open to the hallway, which she pointed out, then took them into the kitchen. "Here's the kitchen and here is my sister-in-law, Clare, who you met the other day."

Clare stood at the stove browning ground meat. "Oh hey." She waved the spatula in her hand at Emma and Jack.

"And here is the kitchen table where we eat as a family."

She looped her arm in his and led him into the hall.

"Whose house is this?" Jack asked.

"Oh, it's Spencer's. And mine. We both inherited it after our dad died. But really, it's his. He lives here with Clare. Keeps up the maintenance and the grounds."

"Why don't you stay here too?"

She looked up at the man beside her. He looked at her like she was the only person in the world. She could feel he wanted to know the truth, but she didn't know how to tell him he couldn't take the hurt away. No one could.

"Too many memories. And this place is so far out, I didn't want to travel so far to work every day. But we're close, so we see each other often. Though it would have been nice if I'd stayed. He cooks so much better than me."

"You don't cook? What about Wednesday at your house?"

She scrunched up her face and looked away. "I

catered. I faked it. Sorry."

He laughed and filled the hallway with the kind of joy she could feel in her soul. He pulled her close and planted a quick kiss on her lips.

"Show me the rest of the house."

She wrapped her hand around the back of his neck and gave him a long kiss. "Follow me."

Chapter 17

Jack

They gave him a room near the middle of the upstairs hallway with light green walls and a double bed with a yellow comforter. The walls looked faded except for the spots where pictures or posters once hung. With an empty closet and light wood dresser, it had everything he needed to sleep, or to avoid the seemingly constant visitors.

He hadn't realized how big their pack was until they were all crammed into the downstairs of the house. The loud murmur of voices moved like waves through the hall. Emma handed him a plate and led him to the living room, where they sat in the last two seats. The room featured an L-shaped couch, a large TV with a stereo system, and folding chairs in any available floor space. Painting, pictures, and other framed art hung on the walls. He recognized her brother and his mate sitting on the couch, as well as the two band members he met that morning.

She placed her food on her lap. He followed her lead and graciously ate.

"This is good," he said after the first bite.

"Yeah. It's Isaiah's turn to cook, and his food is always good. Of course, Tamera, his mate, helps."

"I don't think I've met them." He put a bite of greens in his mouth.

"They're Keon's parents." She pointed to Keon, who used his hands to speak while talking with someone Jack hadn't met.

"Do you always rotate who cooks?"

"We do. Well, we have volunteers that are on rotation. We don't make people cook who can't."

"Like you?"

"Exactly like me. I'm lucky my best friend, my brother, and his mate can cook so well. If I need a home cooked meal, I pick up the phone and beg."

"I'm not a bad cook." He winked at her. "I couldn't feed this many people, but I could feed you."

She lifted one side of her mouth in what he'd come to know as her signature smirk. "Are you flirting again?"

"Of course."

Her cheeks flushed with pink as she looked down at her food and ate again. "I'll be with the pack tonight. Clare will be here, as well as Maggie."

He nodded. It made sense they would have someone monitor him. "Okay."

"Don't try anything." She nudged his shoulder with

hers. "Maggie knows more about witchcraft than anyone I know. And Clare can stop anyone where they stand without a single touch."

"Are all your friends dangerous?"

She smiled brightly at him. "Yes. Of course."

He cleared his throat, took a bite, and studied the art around the room.

"What's that, uh, an art piece?" He pointed to one on the left of the TV. It looked like a chunk of wood in a frame.

Emma looked and narrowed her eyes, then shot the look straight at her brother, who grinned from ear to ear. Clare laughed into her mate's shoulder.

"That," Spencer said, "is a piece I like to call 'My Sister is a Badass.'"

"I thought I told you to take it down." Emma growled under her breath.

"I did. Then I found a new place to put it. You can't tell me what to do." Spencer stuck his chest out like a rooster strutting.

Jack squeezed Emma's arm. He enjoyed seeing her interacting with the people she loved. "What's that about?"

She sighed and looked away from him. "I might have broken the kitchen table a few months ago."

He tried to stop from reacting, but he knew he had failed when he heard himself suck in air. "Oh."

She still wouldn't look at him, and the redness in her cheeks returned.

"I knew you were dangerous." He leaned over and

whispered. "Is it weird that it just makes you sexier?"

She looked at him with wide eyes for one second, then they softened. He couldn't quite read the look she gave him, but it felt important. She shook her head and smiled.

~

Jack

After eating, they all disappeared to wherever they shifted. Ethan told him to stay in the house and ask Clare if he needed anything. Spencer made the point of telling him if he tried to hurt Clare, he'd regret it. And then Spencer would finish what Clare started.

Jack didn't stick around too long after the group left to shift. He considered following to see where they changed and take a peek at Emma's wolf, but stopped short when he realized he wanted Emma to show him. He wanted her trust. Needed it, even.

He tossed and turned on the bed in the green bedroom while he thought about the last twenty-four hours. Exhaustion kept him from thinking about much of anything the night before. Now he stared at the ceiling and tried to put everything he'd learned in order, but all he thought about was Emma.

He could tell within the first few hours after his capture that the pack considered her important. Even if she didn't notice, he watched Ethan glance at her before making some of his decisions. Not all the decisions, but enough to show Jack Emma's importance to the pack.

She also went out of her way to procure the antidote for him. He wouldn't know if it worked until next month, but when it came right down to it, he trusted her. Questions raced through his mind. Would she ask him to stay? Would she come with him if he asked her to leave her pack and her job? And if they found a way to be together, how long would it last before she found her true mate? Could he watch her walk away?

He rolled over on his side. Walking away from her after this past week would prove difficult. If they stayed together longer, his heart would break when she left for good. Letting their relationship die now might be for the best. But grasping onto any amount of love and happiness, no matter how long or how much it might hurt in the future, would be worth it. Right?

After some time, he fell into a fitful sleep. He awoke to the feeling of someone sliding behind him in bed. He turned his head.

"Shh," Emma said. "Go back to sleep."

"What time is it?"

"Around three am."

"Shouldn't you be with your pack?"

Her nose nuzzled the back of his neck. "I'm right where I should be."

He turned to face her and kissed her forehead. "Okay."

She pulled him close and rested her head on his shoulder. "You smell good." Her sleepy voice drifted in the dark room, followed by her slow breathing. He wrapped his arms around her and fell into a deep sleep.

~

Jack

He awoke to kisses on his cheek and forehead and ear. His eyes fluttered open.

"Good morning." Emma smiled down at him.

It felt like her brown eyes stared straight into his soul. He'd gladly let her look all day if she wanted. He reached up and caressed her cheek, then pulled her down for a kiss. One kiss turned into two, then three, then he stopped counting. Her soft lips felt perfect. He kissed her slowly and tried to put every ounce of his feelings into it. It might not be love, but he didn't want to let her go. Whatever they had felt precious. Their hands explored each other's bodies, but he didn't take his mouth off hers. He wanted to kiss her all day, to hold her close.

She pulled away too soon and put a finger to his lips as he tried to follow her. "We need to stop."

"Why?" he asked and kissed her finger.

"We missed breakfast for sure, but also because we have things to do today."

"The only thing I have to do today is lay here and hold you." It might not be fair for him to say that, but at the moment, he didn't want to fight fair.

"As much as I want to lie here and make out in my old bedroom, you need to speak to Ethan before you're allowed to talk to Pablo."

"This is your old bedroom?" He raised his eyebrows and looked around. "What were on the posters you took down?"

"Wouldn't you like to know?" She smirked at him, then rolled out of bed.

"Yes. That's why I asked."

She rolled her eyes and pointed to some clothes on top of the dresser that weren't there last night. "Spencer has graciously let you borrow some of his clothes. They should fit okay, even if they are a little tight. The shower is next door. I'll meet you downstairs."

She leaned over to kiss him again, then yelped when he pulled her down on top of him. "You can't escape," he said with a laugh.

She laughed and slapped his chest playfully. "Okay, five more minutes, then we need to get ready."

Her lips met his, and he let himself sink into the bliss that was Emma.

~

Jack

Jack sat in a plush chair in the study. When Emma showed him around the house the day before, she didn't show him this one, nor did he see the door for it. She told him that the room held special books, so the local coven enchanted it. If you don't know about the room, you can't find it. He bet there were books in that room he had only heard of, and he desperately wanted to read them.

Emma sat in the room with him. He squinted, trying to read the spines of some of the books, to no avail. So, he sat back and looked at the fancy desk and chairs designed for the avid reader.

He turned toward Emma. "How many books are in your collection?"

"Hum…" She tapped her chin with a finger. "Maybe two thousand?"

"Wow. Are they all about the supernatural?"

"You're really interested, huh?"

"Well, it's my job. The more I learn about the people I come in contact with, the better off the situation. I can't work with people if I'm not willing to learn more about them. Of course, an open dialogue works best, but having a foundation gives me a leg up."

"So, you're really just a mediator?"

"Yes. I don't want anyone to get hurt if I can help it. I know how to fight as well. Some people are just hostile and refuse to sit at the table."

"Which groups are the worst about compromise?"

She leaned forward and intently watched him. He loved it when people were interested in what he had to say and for that person to be Emma made it even better.

"Humans. Humans get scared and don't want to work with the creatures of their nightmares, even when proven to be harmless."

"Ah. Humans. Sounds about right."

The door to the study opened and Ethan walked in with Isaiah; the man who cooked dinner the night before, Pablo, and a lady with short blonde hair.

Ethan and Pablo sat down in front of Jack. The blonde lady stood behind Pablo with her hands on his shoulders. Isaiah leaned against the desk as if that were his spot.

Jack remembered when he first met Pablo. He had short hair and an expressive, sad face. Now, the man's hair reached his shoulders, and he stared at Jack passively. He almost thought they brought in a doppelgänger.

Every time Pablo's leg shook, the woman behind him squeezed his shoulders, and he stopped. She looked ready to jump over everyone and rip Jack to shreds. If looks could kill, Jack would be dead before Pablo sat down.

"Pablo, it's good to see you," Jack said. "Thank you for agreeing to speak with me."

"Why do you want to talk to me?" Pablo's face remained blank.

Jack took a deep breath. "After you stopped texting me back, I assumed you wanted to cut contact. Remember the guy, Chuck, that found you before you left? He saw me, and I figured you didn't want him to find you again through me. So I stopped messaging you. And then Dakota disappeared."

Pablo's eyes flickered for a second. "When did he disappear?"

"About a month after you stopped responding to my calls."

The silence that followed made Jack squirm a bit in his seat. He looked around the room to find everyone waiting for him.

"After Dakota disappeared, I began calling around to the different supernatural communities we were friendly with. A disturbing fact began to unfold from all the packs. One or two of their members had disappeared over the last year. It's not unheard of for werewolves to pack up and leave without saying anything, but the numbers were disconcerting. The people missing were established in the community. When I talked to Rod down in Columbia, he told me you never showed up."

"I did show up. And he's the one who kidnapped me." Pablo's passive face disappeared. He looked fierce, ready for battle.

"What?" Jack said. "I'm sorry, that's hard to believe. It's going to take me a minute to wrap my head around Rodney doing something like that." Jack was confused by Pablo's statement. He and Rod had been friends for around ten years. Sure, he wasn't the leader of the Columbia pack, but he acted as their outreach guy. It would give him the opportunity to grab random wolves coming into the area.

"Rodney?" Pablo frowned. "His name is Rodrick."

"What? It's Rodney. I distinctly remember teasing him about his driver's license picture."

Pablo's eyebrows scrunched together. "What does Rodney look like?"

Jack looked over at Emma, who nodded. "He's shorter than you. Maybe five eight? He's strong but has a bit of a belly. And he has short hair like Mr. Isaiah." He pointed to the man leaning on the desk. "He had a huge afro in his license picture, in case you were wondering."

Pablo's eyes widened and looked over his shoulder at the lady standing there. Her mouth hung open like she'd said 'oh.'

"I spoke with a man named Rodrick Kahn. He's at

least six feet tall. Very fit. Pale skin, short brown hair.”

"I am so sorry. I should have given you a description of Rodney before you left. What happened after you were taken?" Jack paused. "If you don't mind telling me."

Jack sat and listened while Pablo spoke about his experience inside Cernunnos's lab. The more Pablo spoke, the greener Jack felt. Being in a cage was bad enough, but knowing he endured experimentation as well broke his heart. Time passed slowly as he listened to his friend's story. Injections, operations, and his descriptions of those trapped with him filled him with sorrow and then rage.

The Brotherhood knew Cernunnos was experimenting, but they only had vague details. The more Pablo talked; the more upset he became. Jack watched Pablo's leg shake and no amount of shoulder squeezing could stop it.

"Pablo," Jack interrupted him. "You don't need to continue if you don't want to. I do have some questions if you don't mind answering them."

"I don't mind," Pablo said.

"Do you remember seeing my friend Dakota there?"

Pablo shook his head. "No. But I don't really remember what he looks like, anyway."

Jack asked Ethan for his phone, then pulled up Dakota's photo. "This is what he looks like."

"No. I didn't see him."

"And how many other captives did you see?"

"There were only ten of us that I know of. I could only see four others but could make out at least five other voices."

"Do you know why they were experimenting?" Jack almost whispered the question.

"At first, I thought they were trying to find a way to strip us of our wolf or whatever supernatural essence we had. But when I confronted Rodrick when we went back, he told me his plan wasn't to get rid of magic, but to take it all for himself. He was looking for a way to absorb our supernatural abilities. All of them."

"And after. Did you have any other side effects?"

"Besides shifting at will now?"

"Yes." Jack wondered if Cernunnos planned for that to happen. It didn't sound quite like a side effect.

"No. And actually, Rodrick pulled it out of me. He could control me and my shift until Hayley snapped me out of it."

"The Hayley you pined after when you lived with me?"

The blonde bent over and looked at Pablo. "You pined after me?" Then kissed his cheek.

"Well, it's nice to meet you, Hayley. He only had wonderful things to say about you." Jack nodded at the blonde, then looked back at Pablo. "And you can now shift at will? That's interesting."

"We don't quite understand why," Ethan said. "Pablo is working closely with someone from the local coven to see if they can understand how it happened and if we can duplicate it."

"Do you think the werewolves that were made would want to shift any time they wanted?" Jack asked. Giving people that option when they might not have control over it might pose a tremendous risk.

"Not all of them." Ethan looked over at Isaiah. "But some have expressed interest in the idea if we figure it out. Mostly because of all the fighting our pack has done lately. It's easier to fight untrained with teeth than a sword."

"Do you have any more questions?" Pablo asked as he stood on shaky legs and leaned on Hayley for support. It was clear he didn't want to answer any more questions.

"I do, but I now want to know how you reconnected with Hayley."

"He came back, found out I became a werewolf, then groveled." Hayley smiled at her mate.

"That's the short version." Pablo laughed. "We need to go check on our cat now. But we'll be back before the moon tonight."

"Pablo," Jack called to him. "Thank you again."

Later that night, after the wolves left for the shift, Jack looked out the window of Emma's childhood room. He thought back to everything the Brotherhood had on Cernunnos. They had several locations; the information insinuated each location contained a test lab. What else were they doing to the kidnapped werewolves, and how many other types of supernatural beings did they touch?

Chapter 18

Emma

The cool fall air whipped through Emma's hair as she wandered around the perimeter of the enclosure like normal. It was the last night of the full moon and she didn't know what she was going to do. She hadn't decided if she wanted to leave the pack or not, even though she wanted to stay with Jack more than anything. He hadn't asked her to go, and she hadn't asked him to stay.

She heard Ethan approach before she smelled him. He walked in time beside her. She could almost predict what he had to say, but she wouldn't make it easy for him.

"How do you feel about Jack now?" Ethan asked.

She looked over at the leader who shifted to speak with her in his human form. Out here under the full moon, they did not worry about clothing. She'd been around naked people all her life. She never quite understood why people made a fuss about taking clothes off in front of each other. Though she remained clothed while out with her pack to protect herself from the elements since she couldn't shift to warm herself up with a body of fur.

"I feel confused. My heart trusts him, but my head questions everything. How can my fated mate be a hunter?" She took in a lungful of air and blew it out again.

"I think you're focusing on the wrong thing. He's a man first. Being a hunter is his job, not his entire self. Just like me, being a werewolf isn't my entire self. The difference is he can walk away from hunting, whereas I can't walk away from my wolf."

"What if he wants me to walk away from the pack?"

"Then you make a decision." He wrapped his arm around her shoulders as they walked. "You are important to this pack. Do I want to see you go? No. But I also want what's best for you, more than what is best for the pack. Within reason."

Emma laughed. Ethan might not be the powerful leader her father was, but he was realistic and steady.

"Have you told him? That you're mates?"

Emma sighed. "No. I don't want to put more stress on him than he already has. He's looking for his best friend, chasing down leads no matter how small. I get it. I'd do the same thing if Maggie disappeared. I'm just a distraction for him right now. I can tell him later."

She desperately wanted to tell Jack and complete the bond. He was already under so much stress with his search for Dakota, helping his sister with the hotel business, and being a 'guest' of a werewolf pack. She didn't want to add more to his plate.

Ethan and she walked for another ten minutes, quietly walking through the trees, under the night sky. The wind blew through the forest, bugs and frogs sang, but it still felt quiet. Most of the wolves were probably laying down by now in piles to stay warm. Emma liked this time of night during the full moons.

"Having a mate is never a distraction," Ethan said, breaking the silence. "You think you'll be a distraction, but I know you could be an asset. Help him on his journey. Together, you are stronger. That's how I feel with Donna."

It felt like a stone sunk into the bottom of Emma's stomach. She couldn't tell which choice was the right one. She wanted Jack to find his friend. Could she help without derailing him? She also had a job, the pack, Spencer, and Maggie. Would everyone think she'd abandoned them if she followed Jack on his mission?

"You don't have to decide tonight." Ethan gave her arm a squeeze. "Ever since your father passed, I've tried to treat you more like a daughter. I'm so proud of you, and so is Walt. I know he is."

He walked away, shifting mid stride and trotted back into the forest. Up ahead, she saw the entrance to the underground tunnel, and she headed straight for it.

~

Emma

She slipped into her old bedroom like the night before and stared at her mate. No, not her mate yet. He looked peaceful sleeping on his side, shirtless, with his mouth slightly opened and his eyes shut, blocking out the world. Since he slept in the middle of the bed, she slid in front of him tonight. She just wanted to feel him. Remember his scent. She didn't know how long it would take to find his friend.

She wrapped her arm around his middle, feeling his skin under her fingers. His scent enveloped her as she breathed him in. She wanted to taste him again. See that look of pleasure on his face.

She pressed light kisses around his face, ear, and neck, hoping to wake him. She never talked to him about waking him up with a blow job. Who brought that up within a week of dating? Maybe she should have. So, she continued her soft kisses until she felt his arm wrap around her and he hummed into her neck.

"What's this?" He asked, his voice gruff from just waking.

"I wanted you to wake up."

"Is there an emergency?" His eyes flicked up to hers, and she couldn't help but smirk.

"Yes." She kissed him again. "I need to taste you."

He leaned forward and took her lips with his own, devouring her, sweeping his tongue into her mouth.

Moans filled the room. His hands traveled over her body, grabbing and rubbing her all over. His hands slipped under her shirt and flicked her nipple. She leaned into his hand with a groan.

His other hand found her rear, and he kissed her neck while she squirmed in his arms. She pushed him away enough to capture his lips again. "No. I get to taste you, remember?"

Her hand snaked down his torso, across his defined body, and wrapped around his hard cock. He moaned louder, and she swallowed it down with a kiss, then slinked down his body. She kissed, nipped, and sucked his skin all the way down. Her fingers dug into his skin, keeping him steady as she worked, knowing he'd have bruises in the morning. The tattoo on his side received lots of love while her hands moved back to his cock. She'd ask if she was doing a good job, but he'd stuck his fist in his mouth while his eyes rolled back in his head.

Tortured and on edge, Emma pulled down his boxer briefs. Jack hissed when Emma licked his cock from root to stem. She moaned when she put the head inside her mouth. She kept her hand still and concentrated on the head, licking it in circles with her tongue.

He looked down at her and moaned. "You're gorgeous."

She slid his dick in as far as it would go without choking and hummed. Jack arched up, his fist in his mouth again. She moved her hand around the base of him up and down. He reached down and placed his hand on her head but didn't try to control her.

"Is this okay?" he asked between gasps.

She nodded and bobbed her head up and down on his cock. He bit his bottom lip while she worked. She sucked and licked and pumped him to the edge, then brought him back down. Again and again, she teased him with an orgasm. He would remember her after this.

"Please, baby. Please," he chanted. "Oh baby, baby, God, please."

She brought him to the cusp for the fourth time but didn't back off this time. She looked up at him and swallowed him back into her throat. He came in an explosion, his cries no longer muffled.

She swallowed all he had to offer, then waited for his cock to go soft in her mouth. As she licked her way back up, she straddled him, then kissed him deeply, like a desperate woman who needed a drink of water. Jack happened to be her water. She kissed him and sucked his tongue as she felt his firm body under her hands.

His hands explored her figure as well. He rubbed and grabbed her ass. Smoothed his hands down her back, warmed her legs with his hands. Without warning, he moved her up enough to lap at her nipples. She shuddered under the attention. She could only hold herself above him while he worked. A gasp escaped her when his hands moved between her legs, brushing against her clit.

A long, wide finger slid inside her, his mouth still attached to a nipple, and his other hand held her up like a rag doll. He switched nipples, flicking it with his tongue to where the sensation shot straight to her throbbing bud. A second finger slid inside her. He moved his fingers in and out of her, using the base of his hand to rub her nub.

Words spewed out of her mouth, but she didn't know exactly what she said. He pulled his fingers out, to which she whined.

"Baby," he said, letting go of her tit. "Ride my face."

He didn't wait for an answer. He pulled her over his face and got to work. She felt his tongue lick the entire length of her vulva. His hands grasped her hips, moving her where he wanted. He licked inside her channel like he was searching for honey. His stubble rubbed against her thighs and along her entrance. She swore if he stayed there long enough, he might find her g-spot.

Before she could grind on his face to give him a better chance, he moved up to her clit. Electric shocks shot through her body. He kissed and licked and sucked on her nub. He hummed the entire time, sending vibrations dancing over her skin. She looked down and saw her rubbing herself all over his face. When that started, she couldn't say, but his eyes twinkled between her thighs.

Each nip and flick on her bundle of nerves pushed her closer and closer to the edge. She heard herself getting louder but couldn't care less. Let everyone hear them. Jack's hand brushed over her skin and cupped her breast. One small twist of her nipple had her falling over the edge into bliss.

He slowly lapped at her while she leaned against the headboard and caught her breath. She fell backwards as if boneless, but he caught her and moved her to his side. They lay side by side lazily kissing each other until they drifted off into sleep.

Chapter 19

Jack

Monday finally came, much to Jack's delight and dismay. He needed to get out of this house, but he didn't want to leave Emma. A weekday morning moved faster than the weekend. People rushed for food and ran out the door. He couldn't imagine the stress of trying to make it to work on time after a full moon.

Once most of the chaos calmed down, Ethan shook Jack's hand. "It was a pleasure to meet you. I hope to see you more often in the future. I'm sure you will have lots to discuss with your father once you leave here."

Jack smiled. "The pleasure was all mine."

"Don't forget our agreement. The plan is to blindfold you, drive you out, and meet you in a central location with your car. Once that happens, an associate will erase your knowledge of our location."

The last part made Jack nervous. "That last part

sounds dangerous."

"It's not. Emma will be with you the entire time. Now, I need to go, or I'll be late. I'll see you in two weeks." Ethan turned and walked out the front door and left Jack staring after him.

Two weeks? What was happening in two weeks? Maybe Ethan arranged something with Jack's father. That didn't guarantee Jack's presence. His father did what he thought best for the Brotherhood, even when others disagreed. He knew he needed to be at whatever meeting they planned.

"Ready?" Emma asked, placing her hand on his shoulder.

"Yeah."

They walked out to her car. His car sat beside hers.

"Who's taking my car?" he asked.

"I am." Keon walked up and opened the car door. "Don't worry. I'm a mechanic."

He hopped in the car and drove off before Jack could say anything.

"That doesn't make me feel better for some reason," he muttered.

Emma laughed and unlocked her car with a push of a button. He watched her walk around the car and pull open the driver's side door. She looked beautiful with the sunrise shining through the trees. He wanted to remember her that way with a big bright smile and the light hitting her just right. She looked like an angel.

"Come on," she said. "I've got a blindfold for you."

He rolled his eyes and got in the car. She tied the

blindfold over his eyes and started up the car.

"How much longer are you staying in Savannah?"

"I don't know." He resisted taking off the blindfold. These last few moments would be the last time he'd get to see Emma for who knew how long. "Depends on if Paul still needs me for the hotel business."

"Paul, who was arrested by the police because of public intoxication?" He heard the laugh in her voice. "You know I can look up who was arrested the next day, right?"

He laughed. "I panicked. And my face hurt. Pablo really got me good that day."

Her voice softened. "And if you're not needed for the hotel business?"

"I'll need to go back. Especially with the new information we have on Cernunnos. If they have Dakota, I need to get him out of there."

They sat in silence for a while. He only heard the car's tires rolling on the road. Normally, the silence between them felt normal, but today it felt itchy and uncomfortable.

"Are you okay?" he asked.

"Yeah." He could hear the lie but didn't call her on it.

"If I came back, would you want to see me?" He swallowed down the question he really wanted to ask. She couldn't leave her job for him.

"Of course. I'd always want to see you."

The words 'always want to see you' lightened his heart. He always wanted to see her too. "Can I call you?" he ventured.

"I'd be sad if you didn't." He felt her hand rest on his knee and squeeze. Her hand stayed there until she stopped the car and took his blindfold off.

"We're here. But you'll need to stay here for a moment."

He looked around and saw they were at an auto repair shop named Massy and Sons. The parking lot looked more than full, and he saw Keon walk into a bay and give Hayley, Pablo's mate, a high five.

The back doors of the car opened, and he turned to see Jesi and Maggie climb in.

"Are you ready, Jackie?" Maggie made a face. "I don't like that nickname. Don't worry, I'll figure it out."

"What's going on?" He looked at Emma.

"Jesi will erase any location information you have regarding the pack's location." Emma reached over and held his hand.

"You really don't trust me." He couldn't stop the hint of whine that came out when he spoke.

"I trust you. But it's not up to me," Emma said.

"It's up to me." Maggie grinned wildly, her pink hair bouncing.

"Sorry," Jesi said. "My cousin is... yes."

"I'm so glad you're a lawyer." Maggie laughed at Jesi.

"So, Jack. I'm going to put my hands on either side of your head." Jesi scooted to the edge of her seat. "Then once I find what I'm looking for, I'll say an incantation. Maggie will throw some herbs, and that small bit of knowledge will be blocked from your active memory."

"That's one hell of a spell." He turned to get a better

look at the witch. She looked the same as she did at Spencer's house. This might be the reason everyone considered gleaning so dangerous.

"Yeah. According to my research, only those with the gleaning power can use this spell effectively." Jesi patted him on the shoulder. "Are you ready?"

"I don't really have a choice."

He turned and let Jesi touch his head.

"You'll need to let go of Emma's hand," Maggie said.

He tried to breathe slowly and not jostle her while she worked. He didn't need her to block all his memories. The sound of Jesi's mumbling caught his attention. He tried to make out the words but failed. The next thing he knew, a dusting of herbs fell on his head and into his face.

Jesi removed her hands while he sputtered rosemary out of his mouth. Emma reached over and brushed the rest out of his hair.

"Well, that was fun. I have work to do." Jesi left the car.

"Damn," Maggie said. "I knew I should have taken a separate car. I gotta go. I'd threaten you, but I have a feeling you've gotten that from everyone else. Just know that magic can cover a variety of situations."

Maggie got out of the car and blew Emma a kiss. Emma shook her head and turned back to Jack. He wondered if he should stay for a little longer.

Emma pulled out his phone from her pocket and handed it to him. "You'll need this. I made sure to charge it."

He booted up the phone and clasped it tight in his

hand. "Thank you."

"It's been a weird weekend, huh?" She laughed. "Are you going to tell your dad you were taken down by a girl?"

He raised an eyebrow at her. "I was taken down by a werewolf. He'll be disappointed that someone bit me, though. I'm sure he'll tell me all about how he taught me better than that."

He opened his messages and read through Paul's. "Looks like all the hotel business is complete for now."

"You're leaving now. I know. You gotta find your friend." Emma cupped his face with her hands.

"Yeah. He's been missing for more than a year now. At least we know we're on the right track." He kissed her palm.

"Let me walk you to your car."

As soon as he got into his car, this detour would be over, but he didn't want it to end. They stood outside his driver side door and she pulled him into a hug.

She relaxed in his arms. He never wanted the sensation of her in his arms, of knowing she was only a short drive away, to end. They weren't meant to be together. Once she found her mate, she'd forget about him. Even the thought broke his heart. He would jump at the chance to be her mate. Forever with her sounded like paradise. He needed to walk away now, before his attachment grew.

He gave her a soft, slow kiss there in the parking lot of the auto shop and tried to sear the feeling, this moment, into memory.

He pulled back and ran his fingers through her hair.

"I need to go. I'll call you."

"You'd better."

He climbed in his car and drove away from her, willing her into his front seat. He settled for watching her in his rear-view mirror.

~

Emma

As soon as Jack turned that first corner out of sight, she knew she'd made a mistake. She should have told him and now she felt broken. Tears streamed down her cheeks. Maybe he'd turn around for her. Ten minutes later, she got into her car and drove to work. At least she could drown in the cuddles of adorable animals.

Chapter 20

Emma

Emma sat behind the counter of Herbs and Healing of Savannah. She fiddled with a crystal while Maggie helped a customer. The pink rock dispersed the surrounding light. It was one of those stones she wanted to put in her pocket, but Maggie might strangle her or make her pay double.

The customer finally left, and Maggie leaned against the counter and looked at her.

"Well, have you talked to him?"

"We've texted some." Emma frowned. He left four days ago. "It's not the same."

"I bet. You should have told him you were mates." Maggie started drumming her fingers on the desk. "I can't believe you let him just leave."

"I don't want to get in the way of him finding his best friend. I wouldn't want a distraction if you dropped off the face of the earth."

"First off, I won't drop off the face of the earth and second, Jack wouldn't be a distraction. He'd do anything he could to help, just like you would do anything you could to help. You're just scared."

Emma rolled her eyes. "I'm not scared."

"I've never seen you so scared. I don't even know what you're afraid of."

"I'm not scared," Emma repeated.

"Right. Just like you're not scared of roaches."

"Hey. Only roaches that fly. They shouldn't fly."

"The big, bad werewolf is scared of a flying insect." Maggie gave her a mocking frown.

"I hate you."

"You love me."

Emma looked away but felt Maggie studying her. Maybe she should have had dinner with her brother instead.

"What was yesterday's meeting with Ethan about?"

Emma groaned. "I shouldn't be surprised you know about it. He called a group of us together to talk about a possible alliance with the Brotherhood."

"Oh? A possible alliance?"

"Yeah. They want us to meet next weekend to discuss how we can help each other. It's going to be in Columbia and some members of the pack there will mediate."

"Who does he want to go?"

"Ethan, James, Pablo, and me." Emma put the crystal down and picked up a blue one.

"Not Isaiah or Sally?"

"Isaiah is in charge while he's gone, and Sally is holding a grudge. I don't blame her."

"So, when do we leave?"

Emma looked up at her best friend. "Excuse me?"

"You're not going without me. I'm coming too. I'll be like the coven delegate."

"We don't need a coven delegate."

"Sure, you do. I'd suggest Aunt Sylvia, but she takes some getting used to, which might slow down negotiations."

"Do you really think Ethan will agree to this?"

Maggie shrugged. "I'll just show up. I'll even drive. Make some deliveries in the area. We can share a room and stay up late gossiping about the members of the Brotherhood."

"That won't convince Ethan."

"How about I bring along some spells and potions that will help us learn the true intentions of them while y'all negotiate?"

"He won't say no to that. He might want to bring a second witch, though."

"I vote for Dylan. Or Finn. Or Jesi. Just not Aunt Sylvia."

Emma laughed. "She is a bit uptight."

"I love her, and she's great to have on your side, but she's not good at compromise."

"I remember the first time I met her. I was so nervous. More nervous than when I met Gigi. Then she pulled us aside when we were running in the house and got on to us. She didn't even yell, but I was still so scared."

"Not all power is magic."

~

Rodrick

"Are you sure this is a good idea?" Andre leaned against the wall.

Rodrick sat back in his chair, amused that his second dared to question him. "He asked for a second chance. And he'll get it."

A knock on the door interrupted them.

"Come," Rodrick said.

Gunter walked in wearing a polo with the Cernunnos's symbol and the buzz cut Andre convinced the men to wear. "You called for me, sir?"

"Yes. Why don't you sit?" Rodrick motioned to the chair in front of his desk.

Gunter sat. Rodrick liked the new chairs he picked out for his office. They were large enough to seem like normal chairs, but short enough for anyone sitting there to look up at him. Andre figured that out the first day and preferred to stand. Rodrick allowed it, for now.

"You wanted a second chance." Rodrick stood up and buttoned his blazer. "I have just the job for you."

"Thank you, sir. Anything."

"The new moon will be upon us soon. I want you to attack the Savannah pack again. Set fire to the woods, drive a car into the house, whatever you need to do. Draw the witch out. She can't stop herself from coming to those scruffy wolves' aid."

"That's no problem. I can do that."

"You'll have help, of course. You can take up to six other men, but you will also take the beast men."

"Th... th the beast men?" Gunter sank down into the chair. "Can they be trusted?"

"Yes. More than you. Andre will teach you the commands. Beyond that, be creative, but," Rodrick looked down his nose at Gunter and yelled, "DRAW THE WITCH OUT!"

Gunter's face grew pale as he nodded his head.

"And remember, we want her alive. If you can't capture her, make sure you get a tracker on her. Now go. You have just over a week to prepare."

Gunter gave Rodrick a little bow and scurried out of the room.

"Do you really think that witch is the key?" Andre asked, and not for the first time.

"Yes. She's the heart of that coven while being essentially powerless. Grabbing her shouldn't be this hard." He took a deep breath to calm down. Getting worked up over a human wasted his time. "I want you to follow Gunter this time. If he's captured again, take care of him before he gives them any more information."

"Yes, sir." Andre crossed his arms. "We were lucky last time. He didn't know about any of the programs."

"Don't say it," Rodrick cut him off. "I know what you're going to say. I know it's a risk to send him. I also know he's expendable. Don't question me again."

Rodrick narrowed his eyes at his second, then looked

toward the door. Andre understood and left the office.

Rodrick sat back down and opened the file on his desk. He only needed one more piece of the puzzle and the world would be safe in his hands.

Chapter 21

Jack

Jack couldn't wait to see Emma. He walked around with his head in the clouds after his father told him who planned to attend from the Savannah pack. Honestly, he assumed his feelings for her would diminish with time. Maybe he needed more time, because his feelings only grew. He looked forward to her texts and their phone calls. She stayed on his mind, and he had already made space in his schedule to go see her again.

His group arrived at the hotel in Columbia early afternoon on Friday. His friend Rodney, of the Soda City Pack, greeted them and showed them where they could hold their discussion. They agreed to meet in Columbia as neutral territory, halfway between each group. Rodney and the pack leader Maren would act as mediators, since the Soda City Pack was friendly with both organizations.

After checking in and settling into his room, Jack

came down and lounged around the lobby. He told himself he didn't want to stay cooped up in his room alone, but he lied to himself. Actually, he wanted to see Emma again. He missed the smirk on her lips, the warm brown eyes looking straight into his soul, and the warmth of being next to her.

After an hour's wait, she walked into the hotel. He almost fell out of his seat as he watched her walk past and up to the registration desk. She wore jeans that hugged her ass and a tank top showing her toned, gorgeous arms. Her long hair flowed free, and he wanted nothing more than to bury his head in her neck and breathe her in.

He finally convinced his legs to move and walked over to her.

"Emma," he called to her.

She turned and looked at him with a huge smile that blew him away. If only he could make her smile like that all the time.

"Jack." Emma took two steps, then threw herself at him.

He caught her and squeezed her like this might be the last time they'll see each other. She still smelled amazing, like strawberries and coffee. It felt like her entire body pressed against him. He didn't want to let go, but someone cleared their throat behind him.

They broke away to find Emma's friend Maggie standing there with a smile. "Let's not take it any further in public, children."

Emma rolled her eyes. "You remember Maggie, right?"

"Of course. I'm glad you could make it." Jack shook her hand.

"Like I'd let her come by herself."

"Ethan and the others are right behind us." Emma rolled her eyes at Maggie and pointed to the group checking in behind her.

Jack didn't notice them when Emma walked in. In fact, he didn't notice Maggie either. He swallowed hard. He knew Emma would break his heart, but he didn't have the strength to walk away. He had become attached.

"Would you like to have dinner tonight?" he asked Emma.

Her eyes lit up, then dimmed when she looked over at Maggie. "Well…"

"Of course, she will." Maggie patted Jack on the back. "I'm going to save Pablo from the old men doing old men things. I'm headed to the room. Want me to take your bag?"

"Yeah."

He saw Emma mouth 'thank you' to her friend. Jack looked at his watch. "If you want to leave now, I know a nice place we can go before the crowds start."

She wrapped her hand around his arm. "Let's go."

~

Emma

Emma stood in her hotel room the next morning, gushing to Maggie.

"It felt like no time had passed. We just picked up

right where we left off. Don't you love it when a date opens your car door?"

Maggie pulled on her blouse. "Of course. I also like opening doors for my dates."

Emma continued. "And the way he kissed me good night, I almost melted right there in front of the door."

"What time did you get back, anyway? I fell asleep around eleven."

"I got in at midnight." Emma, already dressed, brushed her hair. "He took me to a place where we could see the stars. It was so beautiful and romantic."

"So…" Maggie put her hands on her hips. "Did you tell him?"

Emma looked anywhere but at Maggie. "No."

"Ugh. You need to tell him, or I will. He'll know exactly what it means. You don't even have to explain it."

"What if he doesn't want to be my mate?"

"Have you seen the way he looks at you? He didn't notice me the first time y'all met at the Gallery Espresso, and he didn't notice me in the lobby yesterday. And I'm noticeable. Bright pink hair. Loud." Maggie sighed. "Besides, if he doesn't want to be your mate, I'll take his balls."

Emma laughed. "Okay, I'll tell him today."

They gathered their things and took the elevators to the floor with the meeting rooms. Emma saw Jack standing at the entrance of one room, and she half jogged over to him.

"Hey." She smiled.

"Hey." He leaned over and gave her a quick kiss. "We

won't be able to do any of that in there, so I wanted to do it before."

"Gross you two," Maggie said. "Wait. There's something on my shirt. Let me find a bathroom, and I'll be right back. Don't start without me."

She wandered off, and Jack walked Emma into the conference room. The tables were set up in a U-shape. Ethan stood beside a tall man who resembled Jack if Jack were older and played wide receiver for the NFL. Beside him stood two women, one tall with dark skin and long, permed straight hair and the other short with a natural red pixie cut.

Ethan waved her over.

"Emma, this is Francis Bellamy, the leader. And this is Yolonda and Naomi."

Emma shook both of their hands. "It's nice to meet you. Maggie is five minutes behind me."

"There's one other person you should meet. I brought my administrative assistant with me. She's the best one I've ever had, which means she probably needs a promotion and a raise."

Mr. Bellamy turned and called to a lady crouched in front of a computer bag on the floor wearing a nice pants suit.

"Regina, come meet Emma, the one Jack told us about."

"Dad," Jack said, mostly under his breath.

Regina wore box braids pulled into a bun on the top of her head. She turned with a smile that faltered when she looked at Emma. Her eyes turned completely white, then she raised her arm and pointed it at Emma.

"Oh no," Francis said and started toward his admin.

Words that Emma didn't understand flowed out of her mouth. Jack flew past her as well, and he and his dad attempted to push Regina to the ground. They succeeded only once she stopped talking.

Once the lady hit the floor, something tightened in Emma's chest. Pain radiated out of her middle, down her arms and legs. She grabbed her stomach and fell. Arms caught her and laid her on the floor gently. The pain was so bad, she shook and jerked.

"Emma. Can you tell me what's wrong?" Jack held her face in his hand.

"Huurts," she ground out through her teeth.

It felt like her arms and legs started to grow. Her clothes grew tight, then she heard the stitches pull away. She stared into Jack's worried eyes as she willed him to help her. Her wolf pushed forward, further than she ever could before, and Emma the human fell back in her own mind, no longer in control.

She lay on the floor, panting. Her wolf shook free of Jack's hands and looked around. Wide eyes stared back at her. Ethan's jaw hung open, and Emma laughed, only it came out as a huff. Her wolf looked down. Fur covered her arms, or rather her front legs. She checked behind her. A white fluffy tail wagged.

Her wolf sprung up on her feet. Emma tried to tell her to slow down, but she didn't listen and fell as soon as she got up. Unperturbed, the wolf stood up again with no issue. She pranced around in a circle, her tongue hung out in pure joy.

All the smells in the room overwhelmed her. Emma had a better nose than a human, but it didn't compare to her wolf's sense of smell. Then she caught the scent of her mate. Deep cedar, jasmine, and vanilla canceled out all the other smells in the room. She turned and jumped in front of Jack. Two front paws landed on Jack's shoulder. Emma told her wolf to stop, but the wolf licked Jack in the face instead.

"Hey Emma, I see you. You're gorgeous." He ran his hands over her head, scratching behind her ears.

Her wolf leaned into his hand, happy to have him touch her. She whined and rubbed her muzzle on the side of his face.

"What the fuck happened?" Maggie's voice rang through the room.

Emma's wolf turned to see Maggie looking at everyone in the room with a pinched face. Her wolf left Jack's shoulder and bounced over to Maggie, jumping up and down in front of her. Emma rolled her eyes, but her wolf wanted her best friend to see her.

"Emma, you need to calm down," Ethan said.

Maggie dropped her bag and put a hand on Emma's head, which stopped her from jumping. Maggie grabbed her face with both hands and kneeled in front of her.

"Oh Emma," she whispered. "You're beautiful. You're a pure white wolf. The snow white wolf. This is big, Prince Emma."

Emma's brain short-circuited while her wolf broke free and tried to get a better look at herself by turning in circles like she wanted to catch her own tail. Princeps Luporum. How could she be the Princeps Luporum?

Everyone had heard the stories, at least everyone in her pack. Just two weeks ago, Maggie and she talked about how great it would be if Emma was the leader of wolves, how easy everything would be. Well, nothing felt easy now.

Her father and Gigi always believe that the Princeps Luporum wasn't just a legend. That it was a leader reborn again and again when needed. They were told that with a single call from the Ruler of Wolves, all other wolves would do as they decreed. Could she really command an army of werewolves? Even if she could, would she want to?

"Emma," Ethan called to her. "I need you to change back now."

Emma wondered how. She'd never changed before. How was she supposed to change back? She shook the questions out of her head and tried to regain control by pushing forward. She managed to see out as if she were merged with her wolf, but when she tried to push more, her wolf growled and knocked her back.

Emma tried three times, each time her wolf knocked her further and further back inside her head. She could only watch her life like a movie. After her third try, her wolf sat in front of Ethan and shook her head no.

He turned to the Brotherhood. "What exactly did your witch do?"

Chapter 22

Jack

Jack couldn't take his eyes off Emma. He normally couldn't take his eyes off her, but in wolf form, she glowed. His eyes followed her as she jumped in front of Maggie and defied the pack leader.

"What exactly did your witch do?" Ethan's booming voice startled him.

His dad sighed. He had stayed by Regina's side the entire time. She had not come to yet. Naomi walked over and kneeled on Regina's other side.

His dad nodded at his colleague and walked over to the group. "Regina is essentially an untrained witch. She knows most of the basics but has turned down any training I've offered her. As for her innate power, she has the ability to look at someone and see what they need to fulfill their potential or to be their best self. Of course, she's told us over and over that being your best self isn't necessarily good."

"A seer of possibilities," Maggie said. "Usually these witches worked as advisors to kings and generals. Of course, the closer we fly to the sun, the harder we fall. How often does she interfere with people's potential?"

"She's worked for me for three years." Francis rubbed his face with his hand. "And this is the second time this has happened."

"But why?" Maggie edged toward them, obviously looking at the witch on the ground.

"The way she describes it is that there are some people whose potentials or possibilities will never be met unless magic intervenes. In those cases, she gets an overwhelming urge to grant what they need. It's an urge she can't control, like her magic takes over."

"She can't exist like that." Maggie frowned. "It's too dangerous. She needs to be trained yesterday."

Ethan's father looked over at Regina. "I can't force her. I won't force her. It's her decision. What I don't understand is how forcing a werewolf to shift opens any new possibilities, much less why magic would be necessary."

"That is a mystery," Ethan said. He gave his group a pointed look that Jack didn't understand.

"I can go take care of her while y'all continue, or rather, start your talks." Maggie walked over to Regina. "If Emma can't shift back, there might be a reason. And we might need magic to do it. Once Regina's feeling better, maybe she can help me figure it out."

Regina started to stir, and Naomi helped her up.

Frances walked over and talked to both Regina and Maggie. Regina nodded and looked at Maggie then hid her lips in her mouth, her nervous habit. Jack always liked Regina. She didn't talk much, but when she did, he listened. Her organization skills saved his dad from the paperwork that filled his office.

He wondered why Francis agreed to allow Regina to leave with essentially an unknown person. Of course, it might have to do with how Jack described the group to him, including his impressions of Maggie.

"Emma, go with Maggie and Regina, please," Ethan said.

Emma laid on the ground and rolled over, exposing her belly. Jack stifled a laugh. Ethan had zero control over Emma's wolf. Maggie laughed as she picked up Emma's torn clothes off the floor. Ethan sighed and sat down after Maggie and Regina left the room.

Everyone else settled in around the tables. Emma trotted over to Jack and sat right beside him, leaning her head on to his arm. He looked at her, and she smiled at him with her tongue hanging out of her mouth.

"You don't have to sit here if you don't want."

She put more of her weight on him, letting him know she wasn't moving. Jack looked around the room and saw almost everyone staring at them. He shrugged and pulled out a pencil to take notes.

Francis stood. "I'm so glad we could come together today. I apologize for the delay. Let's introduce ourselves and get started."

~

Jack

The talks and negotiations between the two groups went smoothly. Jack endured Emma's constant movement beside him. Sometimes she'd just lean. Other times, she'd put her head in his lap. After a break, she jumped into his lap, but he quickly directed her back to the floor.

Emma whined a bit at lunch. She had a hard time keeping the food off the floor, but she ate what she could. Using the bottom of Jack's shirt, she pulled him over to the wall, sat down, and looked at him expectantly. After she pointed her nose from him to the ground several times, Jack took the hint and sat beside her against the wall. Her head immediately made his lap into her pillow.

After lunch, Regina and Maggie came into the room and tried a series of incantations and spells on Emma. Most of them made Emma sneeze, which Jack thought was cute. Ethan tried to use his position as pack leader to force her shift, which they learned he had never used. Emma happily stayed in her wolf form.

That's when Jack began to worry. He rubbed her head while Ethan spoke with the two witches. If he understood Regina's power correctly, maybe for Emma to become her best self, she needed to stay a wolf.

The thought sat like a rock in his stomach. He honestly didn't want to give up on her, but could he continue whatever they had while she remained a wolf? He felt like an asshole just thinking about it. As he sat there running his hands through her fur while she lay in his lap, he realized that it didn't matter. Maybe it wouldn't be a romantic relationship, but he didn't want to leave her again. Maybe he could convince her to live with him. Even as a wolf. He had the room.

Chapter 23

Emma

Emma was bored. Her wolf, however, enjoyed every moment next to Jack. She couldn't blame her. And now she knew how her wolf felt being cooped up all the time. She tried several more times throughout the day to shift back, but her wolf stopped her each time.

So, she sat back in her boredom and considered why she couldn't overpower the wolf. The answer seemed too simplistic. She wanted to be an official werewolf, and now she was. And maybe she felt a bit scared that if she shifted back, she would never become a wolf again.

But she looked at her wolf in charge at the moment and realized that the barrier which once stood between them had disappeared. Once, her wolf could only come so far forward. And now they'd become equals, like they were supposed to be.

That night, they forced Emma to go into the room

she shared with Maggie. Her wolf pouted the whole way and laid in the corner as soon as they entered.

The beds were filled with books and papers. Herbs and crystals were piled on the small desk. Emma didn't pay attention to them. She liked to watch magic, but never felt any interest in learning the specifics. Of course, she'd learned plenty through the years with Maggie as her best friend.

She looked over at Maggie, who sat back on the bed with two books in her lap. She pointed to a passage in one and Regina, who sat next to her, leaned over to read. They both yawned off and on for the next thirty minutes while they shuffled through books and papers. Eventually, they both nodded off on each other's shoulders.

Emma knew she shouldn't, but she whispered in her wolf's ear, 'We should go find Jack.' Her wolf instantly stood and walked over to the door. Before Emma could tell her how to open it, her wolf reached up with a paw and pushed down on the handle. Someone paid attention for the last twenty-eight years.

They left the room and followed his scent down the hall. They pawed at his door off and on for a few minutes until it opened, and her wolf shot straight inside without an invitation.

"Emma," Jack said after the door closed. "What are you doing here?"

They looked around the room. It looked much like hers, only this room had a king bed instead of two queens. She turned in circles, then jumped on his bed, worked her way under the covers, and laid down.

He sighed and sat beside her. "You really shouldn't be here."

She rolled onto her back for a belly rub, which he didn't hesitate to give.

"Okay. I'll let you stay, but I'm not taking the fall when they come asking about you."

She watched him putter about the room as he got ready for bed. Once he climbed in, she moved until she could put her head on his shoulder and she and her wolf fell asleep.

~

Emma

Emma woke up and realized she was wrapped around someone. The dark room didn't help much, but there was enough light for her to make out the face of the man beside her.

Jack. She should have known from his scent, but she felt off. She ran her hands through her hair and stopped and looked down. Her hands. She was human again. Human and naked in Jack's bed because her wolf couldn't stay away. Truth be told, Emma didn't want to stay away either.

The bed creaked a little as she slowly climbed out of bed. She needed a bathroom and some clothes. Once done in the restroom, she walked around the room in the dark, looking for a clock. She finally spotted Jack's phone plugged in beside the bed. With one touch, the phone lit up, showing her it was 5:04 am.

A hand grabbed her wrist, and she looked down to see Jack's eyes on her. "It's still early. Come back to bed."

He didn't let go until she nodded her head. After she climbed back into bed, he pulled her close and wrapped his arms around her.

"You're human again." His hand lightly brushed her arm up and down.

"Yeah. I'm a little surprised."

"I think we were all surprised when you couldn't shift back. Has that happened before? Does your wolf like to take over often?"

Emma buried her head in his chest. "I don't really know what she likes."

"What do you mean?"

She felt him turn and when she lifted her eyes, he peered at her. Her heart started pounding in her chest. This couldn't go on. She had to tell him.

She looked away and softly said, "I've never shifted before."

He tensed around her. "What?"

"That was the first time I'd shifted."

"Emma, look at me."

She lifted her head and stared at him. Darkness shrouded his face, but there was enough light for her to see his mind churning.

"That was your first shift? Did Regina give you a wolf?"

Emma laughed. She couldn't stop herself, so she buried her face in his chest again while she tried to control herself.

"I can't wait to tell Maggie you asked that," Emma said when she'd calmed down enough to talk again. "A witch can't give you a wolf. Well, unless that witch is also a wolf and they bit you."

"Then what…" Jack trailed off. "You. It's you."

"Yeah. It's me. I'm a carrier."

"Really?" He cupped her face with both hands. "That's fascinating. And now you can shift. Or can you? Can you shift again?"

Emma focused and looked inside herself. The barrier between her and her wolf had indeed vanished. She took a deep breath and gave control to her wolf. The shift was slow and painful, but at the end, she looked down to see her paws. Instead of viewing the world from behind her wolf, now they viewed it side by side.

Just as slowly as before, she shifted back into a human. Sweat pooled on the back of her neck and across her body. Jack pushed her hair back and gazed into her eyes.

"I have two questions," Jack said. "One. I've seen your wolf in your eyes before. How could that be if you're a carrier?"

Emma looked down. "Until yesterday, we had a barrier between us. I could sense her, and she could sense me. When I was twenty-two, I watched my father die. A hunter murdered him in front of me. The anger from both my wolf and me shattered part of the barrier, but not completely. She's been showing up ever since then."

"What happened to the hunter?"

"It's probably best if you don't know." She fiddled with the sheets and avoided his eyes. "What's your second question?"

"If you can shift now, are you still considered a carrier?"

She tensed in his arms. "I don't know."

His hands ran over her head and down to her arms. She hadn't even thought about her carrier status. Ethan and Maggie surely had. Without a carrier, they couldn't make the antidote. It felt like a win for Cernunnos. She tried to relax in Jack's embrace and let his strokes calm her.

Sleep seemed inevitable until Jack spoke. "Why did your wolf want to sit next to me all day? Maggie's your best friend, and you've known the other pack members much longer than me."

"You make me feel safe," she whispered.

"Really? I feel safe with you too. I wonder why."

She tensed again and pushed her way out of the bed. He needed to know. She needed to tell him, but she was nervous.

He turned on the side table light and sat up. "Are you going somewhere?"

"Can I borrow a shirt?" She felt nervous and naked. She needed some sort of armor before he found out.

"Emma, what's wrong?"

She turned and saw concern written all over his face. He didn't look angry that she might want to leave. He did look dejected and concerned. He'd never judged her for anything she'd said or done. He didn't treat her differently after he found out she was a werewolf.

"My wolf. She wanted to be near you because you're my mate."

His eyes slowly widened, and air hitched in his throat. "Really?" he asked.

She nodded, unable to speak. He climbed out of bed, clad only in his boxer briefs, and walked toward her.

"Why didn't you tell me?"

"Scared," she admitted. "It feels like we're on opposite sides."

"We're not."

"I don't want to be a distraction."

He reached and pulled her into a deep kiss, the kind you sink into because your knees give out. One of his hands held her by the small of her back and the other sunk into her hair and held her head in place.

He pulled back. "You're more of a distraction when I thought we couldn't be together. When I thought you might leave me for a fated mate."

He kissed her again and walked her back to the bed. "You're wonderful, Emma. I dreaded the day I'd have to walk away. Now I don't have to." He smiled and rubbed his nose on hers. "I've read about fated mates for years, and I know it means forever. I never imagined I would be a part of a pair, but as long as it's you, I'm ready to jump."

"There are still things to work out. We live over three hundred miles apart." Emma let him lay her down on the bed.

He climbed over her, hovering. "Details, we don't

need to decide tonight."

His kiss calmed all her worries. She felt the weight of his body on top of her, and his hard cock on her hip. She arched into him and rubbed her body against his. His moan sent chills down her spine.

Her hands explored his body on top of her. She would never tire of feeling his skin, the soft places, the callused hands, or the scars. One of her legs wrapped around him like it had a mind of its own. His hand followed that leg down to her ass and squeezed.

"You're so beautiful," he said. "You're smart and strong and funny." He peppered kisses down her throat as he spoke. "I can't believe we're fated."

"Believe it. I've been holding back for weeks." She sucked his earlobe, and he moaned and rocked his hips into her.

"Does that mean you're not holding back now?" His kisses made their way down her body, where he wrapped his tongue around one of her pert nipples.

"I don't want to. But if you want to wait, I can."

"Are you worried I wouldn't want to complete the bond with you?" He looked up at her, his head between her breasts.

"Kinda."

His smile released some of the tension in her shoulders. "I want nothing more than to tie myself to you. When you were a wolf, I thought you might not be able to become human again. I wanted to stay with you even then."

Any last apprehension she felt disappeared entirely.

"Then make love to me."

He pushed himself up and kissed her on the lips. "Yes, ma'am."

They ground their hips together and kissed, hands roaming, grabbing, and pinching. One of his wandering hands found her clit, and she bucked into him. A finger slipped inside her center as Emma pushed under his waistband and held his hard dick, swallowing his moan. He kicked off his underwear the best he could. She cupped his balls and sucked on his shoulder, giving him more hickies.

A second finger pushed inside her. It was not enough. She needed more. She needed him. "More," she gasped.

Instead of more, he slipped his fingers out of her and lavished all his attention on her breasts. While his tongue licked one nipple, his hand flicked and pinched the other. The only thing she could do was hold on.

"I'm not going to last." Emma felt like she might explode at any moment. Her hand tugged hard on his cock.

He grunted and pulled off her breast. "Wait here." He rolled off her and rummaged through his suitcase. She watched him slip on a condom as he strutted back to her.

"Emma, are you sure?" Jack asked. "Say the word and we stop now."

She laughed. "Aren't I supposed to say that to you?"

He smiled that gorgeous soft smile he only gave to her. "Maybe, but I'm not going to change my mind."

"Me either." She pulled him down into a kiss and bucked her hips against him.

His hips settled between her thighs, and he held one of her legs up over his hip. She felt the head of his cock slip inside her, stretching her as he slowly moved inside. It felt amazing. She tried to push him in faster, but he held her in place. Once he bottomed out, he leaned over and kissed her soundly before sucking on her neck. That's when he moved.

Her head leaned back. The feeling of his lips on her neck, his cock in her wet heat, made it difficult to think. Her nails bit into his shoulders, loud moans escaped her mouth, and her eyes rolled in the back of her head.

His bites, kisses, and licks around her neck continued even when she yelled, "Harder." He indeed pounded into her harder. She gasped. Her throat hitched, and the moment his hand slid down her torso and touched her clit, she convulsed around his hard cock that kept moving in and out of her a few more times before he panted her name and climaxed.

They both lay there as they twitched through the last of their orgasms and kissed each other slowly and softly. Emma's legs wrapped around Jack's waist, her arms around his neck and shoulders. She wouldn't let him escape.

She wanted to tell him she loved him. But they'd only known each other for three and a half weeks. It might be too soon to say, at least to a human. She settled for nuzzling his neck and humming sounds of pleasure. He eventually slid out of her and took care of the condom. He came back with a warm rag and wiped down her sweaty body. She didn't mind the sweat, especially on him. He smelled extra delicious, and she loved how she now smelled like him too.

She pulled him back into bed and drifted off to sleep.

C h a p t e r 2 4

Jack

A pounding on the door woke Jack up. He looked down at the woman in his arms. Emma. His mate. Never had his heart felt so full.

Her eyes flickered open as the knocking continued. He kissed her nose and grabbed the first pair of pants he could find and cracked his door open.

Maggie and Regina stood in the doorway. Maggie's arms were balanced on her hips while Regina's were wrapped around herself.

"Have you seen Emma?"

He made his eyes grow big. "You lost Emma?"

"So that's a no?" Maggie's eyes narrowed.

"Don't tease her, she'll curse you forever." Emma came up behind him in one of his shirts.

"Emma. You're human." Maggie smiled. "When did that happen? And how… don't want to know the rest."

"It happened in my sleep. I woke up around five, and I had hands and no tail."

"Okay, I'll call off the search, though be prepared for Ethan asking questions. And here's your key to the room if you want to get changed. We have about thirty minutes until the last meeting." She held out a key, which Emma took.

"I told him," Emma said.

Jack tried not to smile too brightly, but he most likely looked like an idiot.

"Did you?" Maggie put her hands over her mouth. "Really? And did you...?"

"Yes. We completed the bond." He could hear the grin in Emma's voice.

"You two are fated mates?" Regina asked in her quiet voice.

"Yes." Jack pulled Emma close. "Yes, we are."

~

Jack

Emma left to get dressed while wearing his shirt and a pair of his underwear, then he showered and got dressed himself. When he saw her again in front of the conference room, he didn't hesitate to give her a quick kiss.

They piled into the meeting room for the final negotiations. Thankfully, everything went well. Both his father and Ethan seemed pleased with the arrangements. They ended in less than thirty minutes and sat around talking.

A shrill sound echoed through the room. Jack jumped at the incredibly loud noise. Ethan pulled out his phone.

"It's Spencer. I need to take this." He stood and left the room.

Emma's phone made the same sound. "It's Clare." She took the call and didn't leave the room.

"Clare?" Emma answered the phone.

Maggie walked over to her and leaned in, obviously to eavesdrop.

"Right now? Who's there?" Emma's knuckles turned white as she gripped the phone.

"Call Sylvia. Call Isaiah. I'll call you back."

She hung up the phone just as Ethan walked back in.

"The enclosure is under attack. Someone is setting fire to the trees. Spencer can see at least eight hostiles heading toward them. He doesn't know about the house."

"Clare just called me," Emma said. "She saw a group of people heading toward the enclosure. She couldn't reach Spencer; he was probably talking to you, so she called me. Says there are a few people in the house. She's in the tunnel heading toward the enclosure."

"Is there anything we can do to help from here?" Ethan's normally calm expression looked tense and serious.

"No. What can we do? I told Clare to call Isaiah and Sylvia."

"Isaiah is already there. Sylvia might not make it in time." Ethan started pacing.

Jack watched his father and the rest of the

Brotherhood look at each other. He knew his father wanted to offer suggestions. But what suggestions were there?

"Teleport." Maggie spoke up. "I can teleport a handful of you. If Regina can help me, that is. Otherwise, it will take too long."

Regina nodded. "Of course."

"Y'all figure out who's going while we get the materials." She grabbed Regina's wrist and ran out of the room.

Ethan stood in front of his wolves. "Me, Emma, and James are going. Pablo, you stay here with Maggie."

"I'll go," Jack said.

"I'll go as well," Yolonda added.

Jack nodded. Yolonda could fight better than anyone in the Brotherhood.

"Are you sure?" Ethan asked. "I don't know the situation we are walking into. It could be deadly."

"We're allies now. And I volunteered. I'm sure." Jack stared straight into Ethan's eyes.

"I volunteered too. You don't have to worry about us." Yolonda smirked and pulled a long sword out of her purse.

"I need that bag," Emma said. "Let me go grab my sword. You need anything, Ethan? James?"

"We have our weapons," Ethan said. "Hurry."

Jack followed her out of the room to grab his supplies as well. He normally tried to walk into a situation with defensive weapons instead of offensive ones, but he'd have to switch it up today. From the bottom of his suitcase, he grabbed his five-inch knife, a tranq pistol, and his enchanted short sword, whose handle extends to become a glaive at the push of a button. He hid everything the best he could on his body and made his way through the hotel.

The tables were all pushed against the wall when he walked back into the room. Regina and Maggie stood in the middle, creating a circle with herbs from a bag. He couldn't name any of the herbs in the mixture. He stood next to Emma and watched.

"I'll go first," Ethan said. "Next James, then Emma, Yolonda, and Jack."

"We have just enough to send five of you," Maggie said, looking at the group. "You'll stand in the circle while Regina chants the spell, then you'll feel a rush of wind blow around you. When you feel the ground hit your feet, you can walk. We'll give you one minute to move to let the next person through. The position should be close to or inside the enclosure. Are you ready?"

Ethan looked over at the group ready to leave. They all nodded to him.

"It looks like we're ready." Ethan held out his hand. Maggie and Regina shook it.

"Alright, step into the circle. Don't disturb the herbs."

Jack watched with fascination. He'd seen magic before, but never anything this powerful. Regina looked a little pale, but Maggie squeezed her arm and nodded at her. Regina then turned toward Ethan, who stood inside the circle and lifted her hands in the air. Maggie held up a notebook that the other witch read from.

Regina read,

"Move this person before my eyes,
Ethan Rathor across the divide;
Follow my will, follow his desire,
One step into many, oh goddess abide.

To Old Moss Pack lands, he goes
We ask the universe to bend;
Let him stand, let him leave,
His mind, his body, his soul I send.
In Goddess's name, so mote it be."

In a flash of magical firelight, he'd disappeared. Jack could barely breathe. A hand rubbed his back, bringing him back to reality. Emma gave him a soft smile.

"It's safe. I promise."

He nodded. He trusted her.

His father cleared his throat. "I received a text from Ethan. He made it."

James stepped forward into the circle of herbs. The process repeated, only this time he noticed that all the herbs disappeared with James. Maggie began placing another circle on the ground. Emma leaned over and kissed him.

"I'll wait for you." Emma smirked at him.

In a matter of seconds, she'd vanished like the others. Yolonda stepped forward like she did this every day. She looked almost bored. Jack stepped forward once

Yolonda left. He took a deep breath and waited. The burst of wind around him almost took his breath away. He landed with a thud, like he'd jumped down from the fifth step. His stomach turned a bit, but he looked out through the trees in front of him. He could see a large fence, part of it torn down, and trees on fire. He could see wolves fighting what looked like soldiers at the fallen fence line.

"We need to get down from here." Emma pulled him away from his landing spot, and he noticed they stood on top of a one-story building. "Here's the ladder."

She then jumped off the building and landed in a low squat like she jumped off buildings for a living.

Chapter 25

Emma

Emma watched the battle ahead while Jack climbed down the ladder. Spencer and Isaiah fought as a team against who looked like the leader. In fact, he looked like the guy they sent back last time. She spotted Wes's calico colored wolf jump on top of another man. With Isaiah and Wes both shifted, Clare must have sung "Least of My Kind" to them to force their shift. Ethan and James also shifted and entered the fray.

Fire burned through the trees. It made a bad situation worse. The most imposing figure held a long sword, which raked across a man's stomach.

"Yolonda is fierce." Emma pulled out her short sword. "Let's go."

They charged through the trees. Emma headed toward Wes. A shrill sound turned her attention away. The man fending off Spencer and Isaiah held a device to his lips. He blew again, making that same sound.

A growl rumbled through the forest, followed by something running or somethings running. Stealth was not its goal. Through the trees, Emma saw wolves running forward, only they looked bigger than an average wolf. Once they breached the trees, she gasped.

Five wolves ran toward them on their hind legs. It looked like they were stuck between human and wolf. Arms like a human's were covered in fur with sharp claws at the end. Wolves' legs held them upright. They had the head of a wolf, red glowing eyes, and a tail. It looked like every bad werewolf movie she'd ever watched. And five of them hurtled their way.

Emma changed direction and headed to the wolf at the end. In order to defeat these monsters, they would need to be separated. She swung her sword at the creature's legs, and it jumped back. They circled each other. The wolf person's movements were jerky, like they did not have efficient spatial awareness.

Another shrill sound echoed through the forest and the creatures attacked in earnest, like they found their confidence. She jumped back and cut its arm with her sword. She made shallow cuts on the creature's arms and legs, receiving the same in return. Something about them made her stop short of a deeper cut.

Ethan's voice carried through the battlefield. "Don't kill them. They must be experiments."

Then it clicked. Of course, they were experiments. You couldn't stop a change mid-way without magic, and they didn't feel like magic. How would they be able to counteract whatever happened to them?

Blood pooled down her arms and down her sword. They needed to incapacitate them now. Killing them shouldn't be an option, but they were strong. With limited options Emma and her friends might not have a choice. Her best option was to knock them out, preferably hitting the back of their head away from those teeth.

Ethan, naked and bloody, showed up beside her while she kept the creature busy. "I'll take this one. You need to shift and try to call them to you."

"What?" she yelled as she kicked the beast's knee.

"You're the Princeps Luporum. I know you know. Maggie told you, plus you ignored my command at the hotel."

"But what if..."

"Just do it." Ethan shifted back into his wolf form and lunged at her opponent. She fell back and watched. Their human opponents were all down and out, but the half-wolf, half-men were doing their own damage.

She stuck her sword in the ground, then toed off her shoes.

~

Jack

Jack didn't know what Emma was doing, taking off her shoes now. He had to look away to battle the wolf creature in front of him. He may not be as strong at the werewolves, but he still had moves. After the creature chased him into a tree, he dropped on its back, knocking the hilt of his sword into the back of the wolf's head. The creature crumbled underneath him, and he panted on its back. He looked up in time to see one of the half-shifted wolves grabbing one of the pack's wolves by the leg and swing him away through the trees.

The wolf beneath him moved, and Jack jumped back. Before he could continue the fight, he heard a hauntingly beautiful howl.

~

Emma

The shift happened faster than the last, but the pain still radiated through her body. Once complete, she ran to a center position. She didn't know what to do exactly. The bloody scene in front of her filled her with dread. That's when her wolf nudged her as if she had always known what to do. Emma gave her wolf the controls.

She howled up toward the canopy. A haunting sound, long, clear, and oddly deep. She howled again, this time louder. The wolves all stopped and stared at her. Her next howl began like a growl and ended in a howl that vibrated the trees. All the wolves walked toward her, including the half wolves, the hybrids. But as the wolf people walked toward her, they all slowly shifted into full wolves. Once in front of her, all the wolves laid down. The pack with their heads up, the hybrids with their heads down.

Emma sat and looked over at the wolves in front of

her. Jack and Yolonda made their way over and stood behind the group of wolves laying down. Emma shifted back and stood before the group.

"Pack members, shift back," she said.

Ethan shifted first, and the others followed.

"Ethan." Emma looked at him and shrugged.

He gave her a warm smile. "The pack is yours now. What should we do?"

She couldn't pin down the emotion she felt at that moment, so she told herself she'd figure it out later.

"Let's check to see if any of the soldiers are alive to answer questions. Then we can talk to these wolves and see what they have to say."

"Where's Wes?" Spencer asked. His side bled from a large claw mark.

"Fuck. Go find him." She turned and looked toward the building to see Clare peeking her head out. "Clare, bring us a first aid kit and some healing potions."

The pack dispersed. She looked around. Most of the fire had sizzled out, but not all of it. How would she fix that? When she looked down, Jack was kneeling next to one of the wolf people and started petting them.

"Jack?"

He looked up with tears running down his face. "This is Dakota."

The wolf's tail wagged. Emma walked over and kissed Jack on the head.

"Good. Stay with him. Wait, have you been bitten again?"

Jack looked down at his arm, bleeding on the ground.

"A bit."

She just shook her head.

"Help has arrived." A call rang out.

She looked up to see Sylvia, Jesi, and Chuck walking toward them with two men in their custody. Probably the ones who were in the house when Clare called.

Sylvia waved her hand in the air. The fire in the trees went out with a sizzle, sending smoke billowing up into the sky.

"Better late than never," Emma mumbled.

Chapter 26

Jack

Everything seemed to happen at once. People pulled on their clothes. The older lady who arrived with Jesi and Chuck disappeared into the building they teleported on. Jack wanted to stay with Dakota, but his friend nudged him off. Jack understood that Dakota was telling him to go help. He helped Isaiah carry all the dead into one area. Only one of Cernunnos's men who fought in the enclosure lived. Isaiah dragged him over to Emma and Ethan. Someone tied the two men the witches apprehended to a tree. Behind them, Jack watched Yolonda and James carry the calico wolf he saw earlier through the woods like their asses were on fire. The calico wolf must be Wes, who they couldn't find earlier.

The man they brought before Ethan and Emma had on handcuffs and looked conscious. He spit at their feet.

"I won't tell you anything."

"I'm sure you don't want to." Ethan turned to Emma. "He's all yours."

Something flashed in Emma's eyes that Jack couldn't decipher. She nodded at Ethan, then looked down at the man. "We don't have time to force information out of you. We can grab it, just like last time. And yes, we recognize you."

"You won't get…"

The man jerked, then fell to his side, followed by the faint sound of a gunshot. Blood trickled down the side of the man's head. His eyes remained open and blank.

"Son of a…"

Jack turned to see the man who came with Jesi the time before. He thought his name was Chuck. Chuck turned and took off toward the shot. Isaiah followed him. Everyone else crouched low to the ground.

They heard two more shots, and everyone held their breath, looking at each other. Emma pointed in the direction that Chuck and Isaiah took.

"The other men. Someone killed Cernunnos's survivors." Emma looked around the group. "Head to the building behind me. Hide behind trees on the way."

She turned her head. "Wolves, follow me."

Emma waved everyone toward the building they teleported on top of earlier. Jack moved along with her, refusing to let her take up the rear after she pointed the hybrid wolves toward everyone else. Once inside the building, everyone ducked under the windows and waited.

Clare walked into the room from the back with Sylvia,

both carrying tackle boxes and large fabric bags.

"Get down," Emma said, motioning to them both.

They both squatted where they stood.

"Explain," the older lady said.

"Someone just killed three of Cernunnos's survivors." Emma peeked out of the window.

Windows surrounded the upper half of the entire structure. Anyone inside could see all around them, but anyone outside could also look in. Clare and Sylvia made their way to the group and handed out healing potions and simple first aid kits. They bandaged each other up while they waited. Emma wrapped up Jack's arm.

"You'll need to take another antidote."

Jack almost told her he didn't want one. He wouldn't mind being a werewolf, knowing the feeling of having a fated mate, and truly understanding the pull she felt toward him. He wanted to understand her in every way possible and, if that meant becoming a werewolf, all the better.

A beep sounded, causing everyone to jump.

"Chuck said they lost him, but they found where he was set up," Jesi said, looking up from her phone. "Looks like the sniper left."

An annoyed grunt came out of the older woman. "I'll message Dylan. He can set up wards to detect snipers."

"Thank you, Sylvia." Emma smiled at her.

"Chuck and Isaiah are going to keep looking and maybe track the shooter down or try to find out who they are." Jesi put away her phone.

Emma stood. "The danger is over, but everyone stay

alert. I'm going to follow Wes to the hospital in case he can't shift and needs to see a vet instead. Ethan is in charge."

She took off through the tunnel, pulling clothes on from different cubbies as she walked. Jack followed her.

"Do you want me to come with you?" Jack asked.

She reached out and put her hand through his arm and kept walking. "No. I'd like you to stay here and help. Ethan or Spencer will know what needs to be done. I'll come back if I hear he's shifted and made it to the hospital."

He followed her up into the now ransacked house. Emma groaned as she carefully walked out of the front door. With a quick kiss at a car he didn't recognize, she drove off. Jack looked around the yard. Three more cars sat in the gravel driveway. He wanted to go with Emma, but he also wanted to ask Ethan what Princeps Luporum was about. He didn't quite remember. The phrase sounded familiar, but it stayed hidden in the depths of forgotten memories.

He followed a well-worn path to the enclosure and came upon little red flags sticking out of the ground along the way. Once he arrived, Jesi approached him.

"Hey Jack," Jesi said. "Here's a pouch of herbs and here are some pink flags."

She handed him a pouch that weighed at least a pound and a bag filled with pink flags on metal sticks you push in the ground to mark boundaries.

"Look for all the red flags. Sprinkle some of the herbs over the area. Replace the red flag with the pink. When you can't find any more, go talk to Spencer." Jesi turned to walk away, but he pulled her back.

"What's this for?" he asked.

"Spencer marked all the spots that contained blood. Sylvia blessed this mixture so when it's placed over blood, it disappears. On the off chance the police get involved."

"Oh." He peeked inside the bag and sniffed. It looked like a mixture of several herbs but smelled mostly of coffee. "What's going to happen to the other wolves? The ones that were half shifted before?"

"Spencer and Clare are taking care of them. They'll get food, clothing, and a place to sleep. We'll figure out who they all are later."

He nodded, and she walked off. For the next two hours, he walked around the area sprinkling herbs and replacing flags. When he couldn't find any more red flags, he sought out Spencer.

He thanked Jack and grabbed the supplies. "I'll go double check. Sometimes the blood is sorta spread out in an area. Thanks for helping."

He nodded and let Spencer go about his business, then made his way over to the building they hid in before. Ethan and Clare were talking to three men and two women, the half wolf people. They were dressed in borrowed clothes and were listening.

Jack studied the group until he recognized Dakota. He looked so different from the last time they saw each other. His face looked thin, and he had dark circles under his eyes. He stood hunched over instead of how he stood before, with a straight back trying to get as much height as he could and a confidence that drew people to him. Jack walked over to his friend and wrapped him in a hug. Dakota's now too skinny arms hugged him back.

"I found you," Jack said. "I've been looking for you for over a year."

Dakota hugged him harder. "I knew you would. I wouldn't give up hope."

"Follow me, and we'll get you something to eat," Clare said louder than necessary, probably to get Jack's attention.

He pulled back from the hug. "Let's get some food."

~

Emma

Emma didn't get back to Spencer's house until hours later. She ended up staying at the hospital with James. She sent Yolonda back when she arrived at the ER. When Wes's parents arrived, it reminded her of the time when her father had to approach them all those years ago to tell them he'd been bitten by a werewolf and would change during the full moon. Emma held that guilt of changing Wes for years, even after Wes forgave her.

Now she felt like she was in the same spot. She knew she didn't put Wes in danger, but if she'd never bitten him, this never would have happened. His parents sat beside her and comforted her more than she did them. Wes's family was too good. He deserved better than to be attacked by science gone wrong.

Wes would survive, but without his lower right leg.

He had months of physical therapy ahead of him and probably a prosthetic. She got to see him before she left, and he seemed in good spirits, which was probably the effects of medicine talking.

She walked around the house looking for everyone and found Ethan sitting at the dining room table. "Where is everyone?"

He sat back and smiled at her. "After we ate and put the house back together, the wolves from Cernunnos's labs all shared their story. They all had the same ring to it as Pablo's. And before you ask, yes, Jesi made sure they were telling the truth."

"And now?"

"Clare and Spencer are taking a nap. Sylvia, Jesi, and Chuck left. Dylan will be here tomorrow to reinforce the wards. Everyone else is out back."

"Thanks Ethan. You can go home and rest too."

"One more thing. The Brotherhood has agreed to help with the rehabilitation of our guests. I believe two want to stay here for the short term and the other three will go to Winston-Salem."

Emma nodded and walked through to the backyard.

Several people laid on the grass beside the fire pit. Yolonda sat in a wicker chair, sipping from a cup. Emma needed fighting lessons from her. She walked away from that fight without a scratch on her.

Isaiah lay in a hammock. He looked asleep, but she knew better. Jack laid in the grass with the five people she didn't recognize. The hybrids or former hybrids. They had so many unanswered questions. She could safely assume the person lying next to Jack was Dakota. Emma walked over and laid on Jack's other side.

"Hey." Jack smiled at her.

"Hey, yourself."

He grinned, then pointed to the man beside him. "This is Dakota. My best friend in the entire world."

She looked over and waved at him. "Hello Dakota. I'm Emma."

He looked weary, but still tried to smile at her. "Hi. Thank you for calling us back to ourselves."

"I'm glad I could help."

"Hey Dakota," Jack said. "She's my fated mate."

Dakota's strained smile became genuine. "That's great. I can't believe your mate is the Ruler of Wolves."

Emma laughed and looked at Jack. "I'm your ruler too."

Chapter 27

Emma

Jack left a few days later to take care of his friend but promised to come back as soon as he settled. Emma's patience wore thin as the separation continued. Even though they talked on the phone every day, she grew antsy without him here.

Maggie and Pablo came home with everyone's bags two days after the battle. Maggie brought something extra with her. Regina. After speaking with Francis Bellamy and Sylvia, Maggie offered Regina the opportunity to properly learn about her powers. Maggie had a roommate again.

Three of the wolves that escaped from Cernunnos, including Dakota, went back with Jack and Yolonda to get help from the Brotherhood and the local pack in Winston-Salem. Emma, Ethan, Pablo, and Maggie planned to work with the two wolves that stayed. They had a long road ahead of them.

Wes came home from the hospital five days after his surgery. Emma visited him every day until he told her he didn't want to see her face until she didn't look so damn sad. She resorted to calling him every other day. It would take a few months before he could be fitted for a prosthetic.

The full moon would be back in two days. She thanked her father's forethought for putting in ramps and a smooth surface to the enclosure. It would make it much easier for Wes to make his way to the field.

Ethan sat her down a week ago to discuss her new status in the pack. "The pack is yours," he said. "You are the Ruler of Wolves. And to be honest, I've been waiting for you to be ready to take over."

"Why would I take over?"

"You are a natural leader. Everyone looks to you already. I look to you. It was just a waiting game for me."

Emma sighed. "Jack and I haven't come to a decision regarding our living situation. I can't accept this right now."

Ethan pulled her into a hug. "Let me know when you do. If you stay, I'll step down."

She looked at the calendar on her wall. It had been nine days since she'd seen her mate. After dragging herself over to the couch, she flopped down and stared at the ceiling. Her stomach growled, but she stayed where she lay. Food didn't taste good anymore.

Two days ago, she asked Maggie if she could die from

withdrawal.

Maggie said, "No. But you could die from how your withdrawal affected others."

"You ready to kill me, then?" Emma asked.

"Maybe in another three days." Maggie shook the vial in her hands. "What are we going to do about this?"

Maggie made a small batch of the antidote with Emma's blood now that she could shift. They needed to know if it still worked. The potion, however, turned purple. Not orange. Not blue. Purple.

Emma scrunched up her face. "Let me smell it."

She took the vial and sniffed the contents. "You know, it smells like the antidote, only stronger."

"Huh. Maybe it'll work past the forty-eight-hour mark of being bitten."

"Maybe it'll give people the sense of a wolf without the wolf."

Maggie took back the bottle. "We need a guinea pig."

"We need some pulled pork." Emma's stomach growled.

"Yeah, that sounds good."

If Maggie's threat were real, she would die tomorrow at her best friend's hands. Or her co-workers. They'd avoided her at work as much as possible these days. Even the animals shrunk away from her.

Her doorbell startled her out of her thoughts, and she fell off the couch. It rang again as she lifted herself off the floor. She hoped it wasn't an intervention. If so, she'd have to leave her own damn house.

She looked through the side window, then threw open the door. Jack stood on her steps, smiling at her with a suitcase beside him. She jumped into his arms and kissed him.

"You're here," she said and kept kissing him.

"Yeah. I wanted it to be a surprise. I couldn't stay away any longer."

She felt tears fall down her face. "I'm so glad you're here."

She wiggled out of his arms and carried his suitcase inside, and he followed her. The door shut behind him, and she pushed him against it.

"How long are you here for?"

"Forever, if you'll have me."

Her heart pounded as she took his lips with hers and gave him a bruising kiss. "Really? What about your job?"

"I can do my job from anywhere, though I'll have to travel now and then."

"I missed you so much." She drew in a deep breath, then stepped back. His scent had changed.

He squirmed where he stood. "Surprise?"

"You didn't take an antidote after the second time you were bitten?" She swatted at him.

"Honestly, with everything that happened afterward, I forgot."

She stepped up to him and caressed his face. "So, your first shift will be with me?"

He nodded. "I want you to witness the rest of all my firsts for the rest of my life."

"How do I smell?" she asked.

He licked her neck. "Like coffee and strawberries."
"Yeah?"
"Yeah. You smell like love."

Epilogue

Jesi

Jesi walked into Sylvia's magazine worthy Victorian home, unannounced. She lived in Ardsley Park and Jesi swore she used magic to manicure the lawn.

Sylvia filled her home with plush rugs and soft couches. Antiques stayed behind curio cabinet glass. One room upstairs held the larger expensive items. Jesi's cousin Vera once said Sylvia probably partitioned off half the house from grubby hands when her grandkids came over.

The front door opened into a hallway with an open doorway to the left and right. The left led into the kitchen and the right into the living room.

Sylvia raised an eyebrow at Jesi when she walked into the living room.

"Do you make it a habit to encroach on one's privacy without making your presence known?"

"Sometimes." Jesi sat on the couch near Sylvia.

They stared at each other. Neither one spoke. Jesi studied her aunt. She sat with her back straight, her legs crossed at her ankles, and her clothes never wrinkled.

Jesi inspected her nails. "You said Cernunnos has four of the five books."

"Yes." Sylvia placed her hands on her knees.

"You can't wait any longer. You have to tell her."

"It is safer if she does not know." Sylvia glared at Jesi.

Jesi took a deep breath. She would not let her aunt intimidate her. "You have until the new year, or I'll tell Maggie myself."

Did you enjoy this book?

Please write a review or give a star rating. This is one of the best things you can do for authors.

If you want to learn more about upcoming releases, giveaways, my own book reviews, and more, sign up my newsletter at:

subscribe.lucilleyateswrites.com/n8h0z3

You can also find out more information on my website:

www.lucilleyateswrites.com

Also by Lucille Yates

A Bite of Magic Saga

The Wolf's Bite
The Witch's Complement
The Wolf's Return
The Wolf's Song
The Carrier's Dilemma

Standalones

For the Good of the Clan
The Wolf and the Necromancer

Author Notes

This book has been in my head for years. Like a decade. In fact, this story is the one that started it all. When I initially began writing this novel, it quickly became clear to me that this would not be book one.

Many of the original scenes have changed. At one point my main characters were supposed to be in Atlanta. And the big fight came before Emma's physical change.

I hand wrote my original scenes all those years ago. Unfortunately, I have terrible handwriting and can't read all of it.

But Emma and Jack's relationship has remained the same. Maggie was always there as Emma's best friend. And Jesi, as Maggie's cousin, is part of the original cast as well, though she looked very different and had a drastically different job. I like Jesi much better now.

So many of the characters in my previous books have shifted as I wrote the stories. I get a feeling that something about that character is wrong and have to rework the character designs. That didn't happen for Emma and Jack which surprised me once I finished their story. And I still got to include bits of the scenes I'd imagined long ago.

But none of this would have happened if I didn't have readers.

Thank You!

Thank you for spending your time reading this story.

To everyone who bugged me about book four, I can't thank you enough. Your words really helped my self-esteem even when my anxiety took a hit.

A big thanks to my spouse and son who have supported my writing. I couldn't do this without them. The cats, however, aren't as supportive. Please stop playing with the keyboard.

My family (mom, sister, in-laws, cousins) and friends are amazing. I love it when they tell others about my books.

I'd be lost without my sister and my mother-in-law. Who knew that people close to you can be so honest about your creative endeavors? I may not like your comments at first, but I appreciate them because they are true.

And I want to thank my brain for continuing to type 'whip' when I want to type 'wipe.' It makes editing funnier. Brain...it's not that kind of book.

Sincerely,
Lucille

About the Author

Lucille Yates writes paranormal romance and urban fantasy stories. They feature head-strong women, complicated men, and sizzling chemistry.

Lucille lives in a world full of witchcraft and naps. A recent poll from her sister reveals she's the world's 'okayest' sibling. While homophones create endless problems in her author journey, she still enjoys writing the stories that are constantly playing like a movie in her head. She is excited that others will now enjoy them as much as she does.

When she is not writing, she is reading, playing with her son, watching videos, or playing games. She lives outside of Savannah, GA with her husband, son, and three cats.

The Witch's Truth - A Bite of Magic Book 5 is next!